Scorch

Praise for the Midnight Fire Series

"The writing is effortlessly mind blowing. I could not put this entire series down. Once you're hooked, you won't either because it'll eat you up not knowing what happened! And then you'll pick a team like I did and you'll fall in love with all the characters and you'll want all the bad guys to die horribly! Just trust me when I say it really is your loss to miss out on this series! It's a blaze of glory!"
- *Happy Tales and Tails Blog*

"I love and hate how fast of a read this was! I love it because I couldn't get enough of it and hate it because once I finished I wanted more!"
- *I Just Wanna Sit Here And Read*

"I really enjoyed Ms Davis's writing, I was riveted throughout and was eager to see what would happen - there was drama, danger, action and romance that was wonderfully detailed and described."
- *Obsession With Books*

"The only downside to this series, is that it ended. But the ending was beautiful."
- *My Seryniti*

Scorch

Midnight Fire Book Four

Kaitlyn Davis

All Works By Kaitlyn Davis

Midnight Fire
Ignite
Simmer
Blaze
Scorch

A Dance of Dragons
The Shadow Soul
The Spirit Heir
The Phoenix Born

A Dance of Dragons – The Novellas
The Golden Cage
The Silver Key

To my family for their unconditional love,
my friends for their overwhelming support,
and my fans for their incredible enthusiasm.
Thank you from the bottom of my heart.

Chapter One

From a chair in the corner of his hospital room, Kira looked at the steady rise and fall of Tristan's chest. His movements were in tune to the constant beep of the machines wired to his body. They were the only things telling her that he was alive, because every other part of him was still. His mouth was relaxed, slightly open to let each exhale escape. His eyelids were closed, his brows were flat, and the stress-induced wrinkles normally bunching his forehead were gone. He looked oddly at peace, floating between the realm of the living and the dead.

But it was time for him to wake up.

Two days had passed since the fight in Aldrich's castle—one long day of travel from England to Sonnyville and one long day explaining everything to the Protector Council.

Kira couldn't erase the pain in her grandfather's eyes

as she told him that his only daughter, her mother, was truly gone—that a vampire had stolen her memories, replicated her face, and pretended to be her just to fool Kira.

She couldn't forget the wounded look on Luke's face as she explained Tristan's miraculous transformation to the other conduits. His kiss still burned in her mind, playing on repeat, making her feel alive. Her love for Luke had been simmering in the back of her thoughts all this time, and it had finally broken to the surface, blossoming to a strong flame before she really even realized it was there. But looking at a human Tristan, now so fragile and new to the world, Kira wasn't sure she could let him go and make him face it alone.

But most of all, Kira couldn't loosen the knot in her chest, knowing she had let Aldrich free—knowing that somewhere out there he was alive and knew her secret. That was the worst part of it all, the darkness hiding inside of her that she couldn't share with anyone, not even Luke. A wedge of evil had lodged itself in her heart, a little black hole had nestled within her flames, and it wasn't going away.

She knew it.

Aldrich knew it.

And Kira didn't see Aldrich forgetting about that any time soon.

Which was why she had holed up in Tristan's hospital room, waiting with only her thoughts for company. After learning that she had been dating a vampire, the other conduits in Sonnyville started avoiding her. Her grandparents wanted to reconnect with her, but Kira couldn't stand the waves of disappointment churning in their eyes—after giving them new hope, she had failed to bring her birth mother home. Her adoptive parents had been furious when they heard about her trip to England, and Kira had hung up the phone to escape a lecture. And Luke, Kira's best friend in the entire world, was getting impatient. He wanted her decision and she wasn't ready to give it.

So, take away all of those people and who was left? Her comatose, once vampire now human ex-boyfriend who thought he was living in the eighteen hundreds. Oh, and who almost choked her to death when he woke up because he thought she was a demon witch.

Perfect.

Kira sighed, rolled her eyes, and knocked her head back against the wall. She really was in a corner—physically and mentally stuck. And she needed Tristan to wake up right now, before she actually went insane. She needed a distraction, and telling someone about the one hundred and fifty years of human life they had missed, well, that ought to take some time.

Antsy, Kira stood and walked to the foot of Tristan's bed just in time to catch his foot twitch. The conduit doctors had been keeping him heavily medicated for the past day in order to study his cell composition, but the twenty-four hours Kira had granted them was over, and Tristan wasn't going to be a lab rat any longer.

Farther up in the bed, his fingers bent into a fist and then flexed straight in a stretch.

Kira moved closer, stepping next to his face so she could put a hand to his warm cheek. His skin had a healthy flush and a slight tan, which, though natural for a human, seemed unnatural on him. The tips of her fingers brushed his silky black hair, and Kira studied the slightly curled strands for a moment before focusing on his eyes.

They blinked once and closed again, but Kira's heart stopped.

Brown.

She wasn't used to those chocolaty irises yet. And when he blinked again, Kira forced her breath to steady.

"Shh," she cooed while stroking his cheek. The glaze over his eyes began to recede, replaced by confusion and fear, both somewhat muted from his medication.

"Where…?" he began in a scratchy voice, but stopped mid-sentence when his gaze caught the fluorescent light blinking overhead. "What…?" His head tilted and an odd expression gathered on his face as he surveyed the room.

Oh right, Kira thought, *electricity*. It was easy to forget how long ago 1864 really was.

"Please try not to panic," Kira said. After thinking about this moment for the entire plane ride home from England, she had decided to leave their relationship out—to pretend they were never more than friends. It would be easier that way...for her at least. "I'm Kira," she said, "do you remember your name?"

"Tristan, Tristan Kent," he said with a deep swallow and locked his gaze on her, sending a little swarm of butterflies into her stomach.

"Nice to meet you, Tristan." Kira leaned back, letting go of his cheek to shake his hand.

"And you, Miss..." he trailed off, waiting for her last name.

"You can just call me Kira," she said. He had to be introduced to the twenty-first century at some point—might as well start now.

"Miss Kira," he breathed, letting the words roll off of his tongue while he reached for her outstretched hand. Unexpectedly, he brought her fingers to his mouth for a quick kiss.

Kira untangled their fingers, forcing more intimate memories out of her head. "What's the last thing you remember?"

"I was in a forest. Men were screaming all around me. I was wounded, the pain in my leg was worse than any other I've felt. I was a foot soldier in the Confederate Army and the Union had just delivered us a harsh blow."

"Good," Kira said and patted his hand. He didn't remember England at all—Kira silently thanked her good luck for that. "The thing is, Tristan, I have a sort of crazy story to tell you and I need you to just sit there, listen, and try to take it all in. Can you do that?"

"Of course, Miss," he responded before lifting his hand closer to his face. He tugged at the wire stuck to his wrist, the one monitoring his pulse.

"Leave that there," Kira said, covering the spot with her hand.

"But, if I may ask, what—"

"Just listen, I promise I'll try to explain."

Tristan nodded and set his hand back down on the bed. His movements were slow and seemed slightly disconnected from his brain, letting Kira know this calm mood would probably only last until his meds wore off.

"You don't remember, but we've been friends for a little while—good friends. I know a lot about you and I know how you came to be here, in the hospital. But Tristan, I have to tell you something that will seem a little scary." Kira squeezed his hand, trying to provide an ounce of comfort. "We're in the future. The Civil War happened one hundred and fifty years ago, and—"

Tristan jerked into a seated position, and the beeping of the machines grew to a frantic pace. He squeezed her shoulders, digging his fingers deep into her skin.

"What do you mean?" he said in a harsh whisper.

"Tristan, please calm down."

"What year is it?" he said a little louder.

"Tristan," Kira said, trying to escape his hold.

"How is this possible?" He shook her, hard enough to hurt, and an animalistic fear seeped into his stare. "Where are my men? What did you do?"

Kira slapped him across the face. The sound echoed against the sterile hospital walls and she stared at her red palm in shock. She looked up at Tristan, who looked back at her with an equal expression of surprise.

"I'm sorry," she said slowly.

"No, it is I who must be forgiven. Please excuse my abhorrent behavior, I am just… well, I can't quite explain it…confused, scared, lost…to treat a woman so—"

"It's all right," she soothed while taking his hand. "I understand."

"I do not. How did I come to be here?"

"Let me show you something first."

Kira stood and pushed the chair aside. Lifting her palm before Tristan's eyes, Kira lit a small and controlled flame above her fingers, suspending it for a moment. Tristan inhaled sharply, cutting the air. Kira sucked the fire back in and dropped her hand.

"There are a lot of impossible things in this world," she said before Tristan had time to regain his composure. "And I'm one of them, but so are you."

"Are you a witch?" he asked, unable to hide the current of fear and hatred traveling with that word.

Kira shook her head. "I'm a conduit, a vampire hunter, and you were my friend—a good person trapped in a life he never wanted."

"And what life was that?"

"You don't remember because I just cured you, returned your humanity, but for decades you lived as a," Kira hesitated, hating how crushing this word would be to hear, "as a vampire."

Tristan flat-lined.

His human heart had had too much, and it stopped as soon as she uttered the word. His chest fell back onto the bed, while his head banged painfully against the wall.

"Tristan!" Kira jumped and shook his shoulders, trying to wake him up. An alarm sounded from the side of the room and the intercom system started flashing.

"Help!" Kira yelled, hoping the lightly staffed conduit hospital still had some nurses available somewhere.

Leaning over his chest, Kira listened for a heartbeat but there was none. Forming a fist with one palm over the other, Kira pumped on his chest to the count of three. She widened his lips and forced her own breath down the opening, praying he would wake up.

She pumped again.

His lashes slipped open to reveal nothing but the whites of his eyes, and Kira screamed.

"Move, please." A doctor charged through the door, pushing Kira gently to the side. He put his fists on Tristan's chest, pumping, while a nurse jammed oxygen into his lungs.

"What happened?" the doctor asked.

"We were just talking, I was just trying to explain…" Kira trailed off as the doctor continued to work. After another round of CPR, the machine picked up a heartbeat again, and Kira instantly relaxed, trying to slow her heart to the same beep beep beep of Tristan's restored pulse.

"Give him another round of relaxants," the doctor told the nurse, who jotted a few scribbles on Tristan's chart and reached for a shot of fluids. "Now." He turned to Kira. "What did you say exactly?"

"I just…" Kira walked closer to the bed, lightly running her fingers over Tristan's still forearm. "I was just trying to explain how he got here, in this time period. He's so confused." She winced as the nurse sunk a needle deep into his skin. "He doesn't understand any of this."

"It's all right." The doctor, blond and so obviously a Protector, placed a hand on her shoulder. "It's not going to be easy for him to adjust, but these things take time."

Kira let out a loud exhale. "Have you ever dealt with something like this before?"

"Vampires returning from the dead?" He chuckled softly under his breath. "No, not in this lifetime. But I have seen people with amnesia and memory loss, and they recover eventually—forever changed maybe, but people have a way of adjusting to situations that may seem insurmountable at first." He squeezed her arm reassuringly.

"Yeah, I know about that—believe me," Kira said. If

she could overcome the changes in her life—the truth about her parents, her heritage as a conduit, and her role as a half-breed or potentially some angel meant to fall into darkness—Tristan would figure it out eventually. "Thanks," Kira told the doctor as he walked out the door.

"He shouldn't wake up again for a few hours," the nurse informed her before following the doctor to the exit.

Kira eased onto the side of Tristan's hospital bed. Even though his skin had darkened and his eyes had lost their striking blue hue, her Tristan had to be in there somewhere. He would look at her with warmth and love again, and not as a stranger or a threat.

"He looks pretty good, you know, for someone who was dead three days ago."

Kira recognized that voice instantly and turned to welcome Luke with a grin. He stood in the doorway with his hands lazily resting in his pockets and his shoulders slightly shrugged as though he were mildly uncomfortable. When he stepped into the room, he looked down toward the floor, avoiding the bed.

Kira thought the green in his T-shirt made his eyes shimmer like dark emeralds, and she resisted the urge to run a hand over the soft cotton. "Does he still think you're a demon witch? I myself thought the description was uncannily accurate."

Kira rolled her eyes at the playful jab. "You don't want to know what nicknames I have for you."

"Prince charming? Knight in shining armor? Love of my life? You're not that original, Kira." He smirked, looking at her piercingly under his hooded eyebrows.

Kira breathed deeply, releasing a shaky breath, and subconsciously slipped her hand off of Tristan's. "And you're no Disney prince."

"I know," he said and slipped closer to her, gaining confidence with their easy banter. "Being two-dimensional would totally cramp my style."

"Yeah," Kira started but her breath caught when he reached his hand out to run his thumb along her lower lip. Kira swallowed. "You don't want a perfectly packaged princess to run off with?"

Luke moved his hand along her cheek, stroking her skin until his fingers rested at the base of her neck. He tilted her head slightly upward and forced her to meet his stare. "I prefer my pain-in-the-butt demon witch." He leaned down, arching her head up farther.

"Luke," Kira murmured, shifting her head to the side so his lips landed on her cheek. Even if she wanted to kiss Luke, which she did, and even if Tristan didn't remember who she was, which he didn't, Kira was too conscious of his body lying still right beside her.

Luke sighed and pressed their foreheads together, taking a deep breath before retreating a few feet away to the empty chair next to the bed.

"So how is he actually?"

Kira appreciated the genuine concern in Luke's tone, even if it were more for her sake than for Tristan's. "Well, I told him he's been a vampire for the past hundred or so years, and his heart stopped beating and he passed out...so, yeah, not great."

"He still doesn't remember anything?" *Or who you are?* Kira finished Luke's question in her own mind.

"No, nothing. But he seemed a little more in control, at first at least. The nurse gave him a few more meds..." Kira trailed off as she traced Tristan's body with her gaze.

He was fast asleep and not waking up anytime soon, but what she couldn't help noticing was how serene he looked, even with all the confusion. His features had never appeared so relaxed to her, not in all the times she had seen him sleep. It was as though some invisible weight had been lifted, as though he had been freed.

"So what did you really come here to talk about?" Kira looked over at Luke, catching him mid-stare.

He opened his mouth, ready with a witty reply, but closed it again. "The council," he said and let his eyes slip away to the window.

"Which one?" Kira sighed.

"Both." Luke leaned forward, resting his forearms on his knees, clearly stressed out.

They both were. The past two days had been taxing on everyone, but Kira thought she and Luke had taken the brunt of the heat over the failed mission in England.

Everyone forgot that Luke had managed to save all of the locked up conduits in the dungeon just because he had let a single vampire go free—Pavia. He refused to put more blame on Kira by telling the council that it was her demand to let Pavia escape and instead let everyone believe she had slipped away.

But the real stressor, for both of them, was the Punisher Council. Never in Luke's lifetime or in his parent's lifetime had the two councils met in full. Whenever cross-conduit business needed to occur, one member from each council would travel and make the necessary decisions. But a full meeting of all seven members of each council was almost unheard of—and they were meeting today to discuss Kira's fate now that she had completely changed the game by bringing Tristan back to life.

Kira swallowed.

Her hours of peace stowing away in Tristan's hospital room were about to come to an end. It was almost time to face the world and its consequences again.

"When are they supposed to get here?" Kira asked.

Luke didn't need clarification. "Soon, really soon."

"And what did the Protector Council say?"

"They won't let anyone hurt you—I won't let anyone hurt you. But they are concerned about how the Punishers will act, what they'll demand. This goes against everything they know. For hundreds of years, Punishers have been fueled by their belief that vampires can't be saved, that their humanity is gone, and what you did completely negates that."

"And there's more," Kira said. Luke continued wringing his hands together and looked at her questioningly.

"More than that?"

"Well, that's their argument for why Tristan should die—that the evil will still call for him. But what's their argument for me? I told you what that Punisher in the dungeon said. About how he thinks I'm an angel that's falling and becoming an original vampire, an unstoppable force. They'll want to put an end to me before I have the chance to make that transformation."

Luke leaned back and waved his hand unconvincingly in the air, dismissing the idea. "Come on, Kira, that's insane. Anyone who looks at you can see what side you're on."

"Anyone who looks at me can see my blue eyes, or are you that used to them now?"

Luke scooted his chair closer so his knees touched hers. "I see them. I see two bright and beautiful and warm cobalt blue eyes that look like the sapphire heat of a burning flame and nothing at all like the dead cold eyes of a vampire."

Kira looked away, her heart melting a little under his scrutiny. "Yeah, well, too much sun exposure might have affected your brain cells. Besides," Kira continued, not letting him retort with any more compliments—she could already feel the blood rush to her cheeks a little, "they'll say

I'm too sympathetic to vampires because I was with Tristan. Maybe they'll twist it around so it seems like I wanted Aldrich to go free. I don't know."

"But you've never once acted like one of those things or felt any sort of calling like the Punisher described, have you?"

"Of course not," Kira retorted, trying to look angry that he even asked and not at all guilty.

Because, of course, she had.

During her fight with Aldrich, Kira had lusted for the kill, a prolonged painful death, and maybe even for Aldrich's blood. And that was why he had slipped free—why he had the moment he needed to escape—because Kira had started battling the demon inside of her instead of the one burning at her feet. Since leaving the castle, nothing new had happened. But still, she felt the change within her, the slight taint her flames now carried.

"So that's that." Luke slapped his hands together, jolting Kira out of her thoughts. "They have nothing, no argument that makes any plausible sense against you."

"I'm just nervous, I guess." She shrugged.

"The Flaming Tomato is nervous? I'm shocked!"

Kira smiled. "I haven't heard that one in a while. I was sort of hoping you had somehow forgotten about it."

"Forget the Flaming Tomato? You can't just forget the Flaming Tomato—it's too good." Kira raised her eyebrows in his direction and he responded by raising his hands up. "What? I'm just saying."

"So I have Demon Witch and Flaming Tomato? I seriously need some new nicknames…or some new friends." Kira muttered the last part.

"Would you prefer something more normal like…Kiki?" Luke asked, his face a blanket of innocence.

"Call me that again and I may kill you." Kira sent over her best death stare.

"See, that might have actually scared me when your name was Demon Witch, but with Kiki it's just not nearly as menacing." He folded his lips together to keep from grinning.

Kira launched herself across the room, going right for his ribcage with her hands. The benefit of being best friends was that Kira knew all of his vulnerable spots, and it took about two seconds to have him rolling around on the floor begging for mercy.

Tickling—it was totally underrated.

"Kiki…come on…I can't breathe," Luke gasped between giggle fits. Kira pushed even harder.

He grabbed her by the wrists, finally using his strength and size to overcome her. Without her hands to ground her, Kira's balance slipped and she landed on his chest with an *oomph*.

When she opened her eyes, the laugh had disappeared from Luke's face and in an instant, the air felt thicker. She licked her lips, unable to look away.

"Ahem."

Kira rolled off of Luke immediately, jumping at the sound of an unfamiliar voice in the doorway. She looked up to see a well-dressed blond man who she remembered seeing around Sonnyville before.

"The Punisher Council has arrived. We request your presence at the council dais immediately."

"Thanks," Luke muttered while he stood up and brushed his clothes off.

"I'll meet you there in a minute," Kira said, looking back at the still unmoving Tristan.

Luke nodded and dragged the protesting Protector from the room.

Kira walked back to the corner of the hospital room where she had left her handbag and took out the shabbily wrapped present resting inside. Hastily, she scrawled a note on the blank card.

"Dear Tristan, I'm sorry I won't be here when you wake up again. Remember what I said and please try to stay calm. Here's a history book I think you'll like—it'll get you caught up on everything you've missed. And there's a little extra too. I couldn't find the charcoal you like, so I got some soft graphite pencils instead. I know how much drawing relaxes you. Please don't worry, I'll be back soon. Love always," she erased that, "yours truly," she erased it again, "your friend, Kira."

Kira left the package at the foot of his bed and

walked out of the room, hoping she could keep them both safe from the Punishers now waiting just a short walk down the street.

Chapter Two

While making her way to the town square, a strange sense of déjà vu overcame Kira. Spotting a sea of blond heads surrounding the archaic wooden platform that served as the council's meeting center was a reminder of the first visit she had made to Sonnyville. More so, it was a reminder of how much could change in such a short amount of time…and how much could stay the same. Whereas before, Kira was an outcast for the color of her hair and the source of her powers, she was now an outcast for her loyalties and her supposed softness for vampires.

When she reached the top of the long hill, every head in the crowd turned toward her. Weeks before, their gazes had been filled with interest, awe, and a slight sense of fear. Now, some of the conduits had added disgust to that list.

But Kira had been through too much to really care what anyone thought about her, so she just walked through the people, not making eye contact with anyone until she reached the wooden steps of the raised platform and saw Luke waiting for her. Grateful for his warm smile, Kira took the hand he offered and climbed the steps ready for whatever faced her.

Sitting in their wooden thrones were the seven members of the Protector Council. Kira cautiously glanced over at her grandfather, who sat in the center of the group. Like Luke, he offered a warm greeting. The wrinkles around his eyes crinkled in a subtle smile meant for Kira's eyes only.

The other six councilmen were stoic in their formal suits, staring beyond Kira, back toward the top of the hill where their guests would be arriving shortly.

"Have they mentioned anything?" Kira whispered to Luke, who still hadn't released her hand. But she didn't mind.

"No," he replied under his breath. "Can't you feel how anxious everyone is? I think they're too nervous to break the silence."

"I know this meeting is a big deal, but I don't get what the council is so afraid of." Kira looked behind her again, taking note of the stress lines on the councilmen's faces. Their eyes were narrowed and their hands were white with the force of the grips on their chairs.

"Peace with the Punishers is fragile as is, and they want to keep you safe, but not if it costs us our truce. We need to be able to work together."

"So you're saying they're nervous for me?" Kira glanced incredulously at Luke. It was hard to believe this judging crowd was actually rooting for her. He squeezed her hand, but continued looking at the top of the hill, waiting for the Punishers.

"Some people might not agree with your relationship with Tristan, but in the end you proved the Protectors right—you proved that vampires can be saved—and that is something to root for."

"I guess, but—"

"Shh," Luke shushed her and gripped her hand even tighter.

Kira followed his gaze to the black car pulling to a stop at the top of the hill. The whole town of Sonnyville seemed to hold its breath, pausing together until, in one large exhale, the door opened and a red head slipped out. Six more men in well-tailored suits followed the first older man out of the car and they waited, talking quietly to one another until a second car pulled up.

Now it was Kira's turn to be shocked because she recognized the next face to greet the crowd—her adoptive mother. Tugging nervously on the bottom of her dress, her aunt surveyed the vast lawn, searching for Kira.

"Mom?" Kira said aloud, recovering only when Luke shushed her again. Kira glared at him. "But—"

Luke interrupted by nodding toward the car where another Punisher was emerging. Kira recognized him too—

the man from Aldrich's dungeon, the one who had first told Kira she was falling—falling into evil.

"What are they doing here? I thought it was just the council!" Kira hissed into Luke's ear. Her heart started beating at an even faster pace. The Punisher Council was one thing. But the mother she had lied to and hung up on the day before, and the man who had accused her of turning into a vampire? Kira was not prepared to face that tribunal. "My mother? I mean, that is low..."

"Kira, relax." Luke rolled his eyes. "If anything, you should be happy your mom is here. She'll do whatever it takes to protect you."

Kira raised her eyebrows at him. "Hey, you weren't on the phone yesterday when she was ready to punish me for all eternity. Hell hath no fury and all that jazz."

"Enough." The deep rumble of her grandfather's voice silenced Kira and she turned quietly back toward the Punishers, now a wave of flaming red hair making its way through a golden sea.

Stay cool, Kira chided as nerves shivered down her limbs. More than anything, Kira was anxious about her own response. When she felt cornered, she had the tendency to act out and that was the last thing she needed—to give them another reason to think she was out of control.

So as the Punisher Council walked slowly up the steps, making their way to the seven extra chairs set up opposite from the Protectors, Kira took a deep breath and forced herself to relax.

Of course, her semblance of calm went pretty much out the window when her mother broached the top of the platform. They finally made eye contact and Kira knew the meaning of that singular raised eyebrow and tilted head—it meant lecture time was near. No, it meant, "I am so happy you are safe, but now I am going to make you wish you had died doing whatever stupid thing you were doing".

Kira attempted a weak smile in her mom's direction.

The glare only deepened.

Fantastic, she thought and gripped Luke's hand hard enough to make him wince. *I'm a dead girl.*

"Welcome," her grandfather spoke, directing the greeting to the Punishers but projecting his voice enough to include the entire crowd below. "Today marks a momentous occasion in our two histories. Not only have the councils come together in full to discuss the future of our great species, but we have in our midst a girl who has forever changed what it means to be a conduit. My granddaughter, Kira, signifies the best of what we all do. She has punished a great many evils, but protected the thing we all wish to save—humanity. And that is what we are here to discuss—a newly resurrected human life, a vampire who was good enough to be saved—a Mr. Tristan Kent."

Kira breathed a sigh of relief at her grandfather's introduction, noticing a few heads in the crowd nod in agreement. But not everyone was satisfied with his words

Kira thought, as she looked around at frowning Punishers and Protectors alike.

"That is all well and good, Councilman Peters, but we have other things to discuss," the Punisher opposite her grandfather spoke. He too sat in the middle of the row and Kira could tell he was the leader. His red hair was untainted by white or gray strands, but the wrinkles around the corner of his eyes and the slight droop to his skin gave away his age. His features were hard—sharp cheekbones, an angled nose, a sliver of pink lips—and he moved his razor-like eyes in Kira's direction. Already, she could see the difference in the two cultures.

Protectors were strong, but there was room for lightness and love. Punishers were just tough. Like her mother had said months before when Kira had first learned of her powers, they honored mercilessness with vampires and weeded out the weak—a major reason her mother had left the culture so long before.

"Whether this vampire lives or dies is of little consequence to us. What we came here to discuss is the fate of this mixed breed—her life is a danger you have never truly come to understand. When we found her as a child, the deal was struck to let her live so long as her powers never came to fruition. But when they manifested only a few short months ago, we were never informed, and already her soul has twisted just as we had feared."

"Whoa," Kira interjected, shirking Luke's hold and

stepping into the middle of the circle. So much for poised aloofness. "I may be a mixed breed conduit, but that doesn't mean I'm deaf and can't hear exactly what you're saying about me. My soul isn't 'twisted,'" Kira said, unable to resist the urge to use air quotes around the word. "It's perfectly straight, like yardstick straight. You could measure other souls against it."

Even though she couldn't see it, Kira felt Luke roll his eyes behind her and a sense of amusement funneled into her mind through their connection.

"Miss Dawson, with all due respect, you are the least qualified person to make that assessment. Which is why, according to tradition, we brought your only living Punisher relative here to speak on your behalf. I present Ellen Dawson, sister to your father, Andrew Dawson." He signaled her mother, who stepped forward with a curtsy to show her respect.

"We have also brought one more with us as you have all noticed. May I present Mr. Noah Thomas, the Punisher who witnessed this half-breed's questionable behavior and first alerted us of her possible threat."

The man, who Kira noticed already looked well recovered from his ordeal in Aldrich's castle, stepped forward and nodded to the crowd. For a moment, he caught Kira's stare and his eyes trembled, almost as if it pained him to be there. But his gaze shifted away, downcast at the wooden planks below their feet.

Her grandfather leaned forward in his seat, looking strong despite the frailty of his age. "And what exactly are you accusing her of? Other than saving Sonnyville from a crippling attack only a few weeks ago." He looked at the crowd, forcing them all to remember how Kira had destroyed the vampires who had swarmed this town and broken through their defenses. "Other than freeing conduits from the imprisonment of a deranged vampire." He looked pointedly at the redheaded man who was still looking at the floor, unable to meet her grandfather's steely gaze. "Other than bringing a human soul back to life?"

Kira planted her feet on the ground, resisting the urge to run up and land a kiss on his cheek. *Protectors one*, she thought, *Punishers zero*.

"All the proof we need is written in her eyes," the Punisher said, pointing at Kira as though she were some monster. A thousand gazes landed on her and, hard as it was, Kira refused to back down. She looked around the crowd and met the stare of every single person on that platform. There was one thing she could promise them— she would never stop fighting.

"And before you interject, let's discuss her other actions as well," the Punisher continued, cutting off her grandfather. "Did she not partake in a willing relationship with a vampire? Did she not stay as a guest at a vampire's estate? Did she not freely offer her blood to these creatures?"

The entire crowd gasped at the same time.

She might have failed to mention that little blood sharing part before. But it wasn't like he made it sound. Tristan had needed entry into the Red Rose Ball. Kira had traded blood for information from Pavia. And, she had basically been undercover at Aldrich's castle.

Turning toward Luke, Kira searched for some words to defend herself without sounding guilty. But as soon as she looked into his face, Kira closed her mouth. Through the bond, she felt his fear—a deep burn singeing his heart. The tide was turning against her, and she could feel the shift as golden heads bobbed in agreement with the Punisher's words.

"Did she not bring a human back to life?" Her grandfather stood, purposely leaving his cane on the ground—only the strength in his conviction kept him standing. "What sort of vampire supporter would risk her own life to do that?"

"And I will speak to Tristan since my daughter cannot," her mother stepped forward, looking beyond the Punishers to the demanding crowd below. "He is a kindhearted and gentle soul—I allowed him to date my daughter and to play with her younger sister. I allowed him into my home and into our lives. His humanity was so intact that I at first didn't even recognize that he was a vampire."

She turned a slightly softer gaze toward Kira, who guessed that her mother had never suspected Tristan was a vampire until the Punishers came knocking on the door demanding an explanation.

"My daughter," she continued, the pause unnoticed by anyone except Kira, "fell in love with the human trapped inside of a vampire's body, and all she did was what we have all wanted to do—she killed the vampire and brought the human back to life."

When her mother stepped to the side, out of the center of the wooden platform, a stalemate began. The Protectors on one side, the Punishers on the other—both strong in their beliefs, but unsure of where to take the argument next.

Everywhere Kira looked, blond heads were turning to the side, leaning toward one another. A buzz grew louder as the whispers spread around the circle—a cacophony of opinions. But Kira couldn't tell if the rising murmurs were for or against her.

Luke squeezed her hand, sending warm thoughts into her head, trying to drown out the worry. Kira held on, opening the wall she normally kept sealed tight. Like water through a crack, his optimism pushed through, shooting down her veins, lifting her spirits like hot chocolate on a wintry day.

Kira leaned into his body, and Luke brought his arm around her shoulder, welcoming her head on his chest. Without misstep, their heartbeats molded into one. Their inhales and exhales rolled together like a quickly churning tide while they anxiously waited for someone to speak.

"If I may." The Punisher from Aldrich's dungeon stepped forward. *Noah*, Kira thought, remembering his name. She tensed, uneasy about what would come next, and Luke's grip on her arm tightened. The rest of the townspeople shifted slightly, moving as one to focus on this man as he walked slowly to the center of the platform.

One step.

Two steps.

Kira shifted her weight. Something in the back of her mind told her that his words would change everything— would decide her fate.

Three steps.

Four steps.

He stopped, looking toward her grandfather and then back at the Punisher leading his council.

"I was with Kira in that dungeon. I was down there for a long time before she came, just praying for a miracle— just praying someone would come save me." He focused his attention on Kira—the green in his eyes was forced back by the wave of yellow-orange flames fanning out from his pupils.

"At first, I admit, I thought she was a vampire come to torture me. I met her blue eyes with defiance. But then, she lit a fire so hot it burned the pain from my limbs, seared closed my cuts and somehow healed me. And not only me, but every other conduit trapped down there. I believed she was our savior, and I owe her my life." He nodded, silently thanking Kira in a way he never had before. She accepted it cautiously, just waiting for the huge "but" in his story.

He turned away from the Protectors, finally meeting the gazes of the redhaired council he had walked in with.

"But," he said. *Here we go*, thought Kira—it was almost painful for her to hold an eye roll back. What was it going to be? How she gave blood to Pavia? How she begged for memories of her mother?

"But there is one thing that scares me about this girl, something I would not bring up if the situation were not so dire. She is good, completely good down to the core. So good in fact, that destroying evil things feels just. Unlike Punishers, who kill for the job, because it is what we were put on this earth to do, Kira kills for the vindication it brings, for the sense of rightness that settles inside of her heart. And on a normal conduit, that would not be a problem. But she is not normal. She is two halves rejoined, an original. And every time she lusts for the kill, she falls unknowingly closer toward the darkness. We all know the histories, the stories that were passed down by our ancestors no matter what sort of conduit you are. An angel cannot fall, because if she does, no one on this earth would be strong enough to stop her."

The silence following his speech was like a dagger plunging into Kira's chest, stealing both her breath and her words. He was right—he knew it, and the other conduits seemed to know it as well.

The heat from their stares scorched her skin, burning with accusations. She stepped back as if punched in the gut, not knowing where to look or how to escape the scrutiny. But worse, she couldn't run away from the part of her that couldn't help but ask if maybe he was right, if maybe it was the truth in his words that really stung.

And all of a sudden, that little speck of darkness burrowed in the deepest crevice of her heart slivered out, expanding just enough to draw Kira's notice. Two days had passed since Aldrich's castle—two days of denial. But now, in front of an entire town searching for explanations, Kira couldn't hide.

A filmy oil slipped silently through her veins, shrouding her light, casting shadows over her power. The black ghost clinging to her heart expanded, pushing her always-churning flames to the side, forcing its way through. The darkness was begging for release, daring her to give in. It was almost too tempting—an entire town of vulnerable conduits—something no vampire would give up, an opportunity the evilness clinging to Kira couldn't pass up.

Subconsciously, she licked her lips. Her eyes began to glow a bright sky blue devoid of any hint of yellow and she leaned forward on her toes, a body ready to pounce.

The part of Kira still together, still connected to the sun, fought back. She clenched her fists, a movement only Luke could feel as close as they were. He looked down at her, mistaking it for fury. But Kira knew better, and she squeezed her fingers, using her nails to cut deep gashes in her palms.

As always, the pain shocked her back into control. Her flames broke through the sticky tar hardening in her limbs, forcing a retreat. The fire rushed forward and her hands faintly glowed as her powers took control, healing the cuts.

"Kira." Luke nudged her. For once, he couldn't read exactly what was going on in her mind. He thought her anger was making her lose it.

She ignored Luke and stepped forward, closer to Noah. Pulling her flames up around her heart, Kira pushed the darkness back into hiding—searing the edges and trapping it once more.

"And what would you do to prevent that?" she asked him. Part of her was curious, but part of her knew that getting angry was the only way to make her flames burn strong enough to keep her conduit-side in control.

"Anything," he responded coolly.

"Will you kill me?" Kira whispered. He didn't say anything but leveled an unyielding gaze on her. "So that's it then?" She shook her head, looking back to the razor sharp eyes of the Punisher leader. "That's the big plan? To kill me?" He shifted his gaze to the floor, breaking slightly under Kira's scrutiny. The silence spoke loudly enough.

The conduits kept their gazes locked on Kira.

"Have you even thought of all the good I could do?" she asked, still refusing to give this Punisher a break. Instead, Kira challenged him, walking closer to his sturdy wooden chair. He had nowhere to move, no way to escape. Her fire settled in, rumbling like a volcano ready to explode. Flames licked the underside of her palms, wishing for release.

The image of Tristan popped into her head—his face fast asleep and free of the sharp-edged stress lines normally digging deep into his skin. She had saved him—she had done that with her conduit powers, with her fire. And what if there were others like him out there? More vampires who wanted to be free of the curse? Would all of these people just turn their backs out of fear—was the unknown really so scary?

All Kira knew was the unknown, her life was uncharted territory. And yes, it was scary, but it was also exhilarating to write her own fate.

"I saved one vampire—I can save more. Who knows what we can do? Maybe I can teach you how to heal them, how to bring the humanity back to a vampire who wishes to be saved. We can make a real difference. We can forever alter the scales and take control back from the vampires who completely outnumber us. All you need to do is give me a chance to prove myself, just one chance."

"Well said," Kira's grandfather interjected, using his deep rumble to catch the attention of the crowd and cut

Kira off while she was still ahead. And Kira sensed it—the slightly favorable note playing faintly through the air—the Protectors were still on her side...for now. And the idea that she wasn't alone finally calmed Kira, letting her blood cool off and her flames retreat.

"We have all been presented with a lot of questions and very few answers," her grandfather continued. "I for one would like a night to discuss today's events with my fellow council members—a chance to regroup and figure out how we can meet in the middle to make a united decision."

He stepped off of his throne, reaching to the side for the wooden cane camouflaged against the chair leg. Without looking back, he shuffled to the edge of the platform and stopped right before the first step. Putting his hand out, palm facing the sun and the majority of the townspeople, he said, "May the sun shine down upon you for all of your days."

"May it protect you until the end," everyone— Protectors and Punishers, councilmen and laymen, and even Kira—responded.

With the traditional closing words spoken, the mood around the square visibly relaxed. Councilmen stepped off of their chairs to their waiting families below. Children began to run around. Friends began to gossip. The grassy lawn began to clear as people made their way home. And Kira felt she could finally breathe again, like the air was somehow fresher. It might have been a shaky victory, but hey, beggars couldn't be choosers.

So, following Luke, Kira walked off the platform and took a deep breath, unsure of where to go.

There was always Luke's home, but his sister was watching Kira like a hawk. Or the hospital, if Tristan was awake enough to try to face his new reality again. But no, Kira realized what she needed to do. Her mother was waiting somewhere in the crowd, armed with either a warm hug or a harsh lecture. Kira was ready for both.

"Have you seen my mom?" she asked Luke, confused about how any redheaded woman would be so hard to find in this crowd.

"Your mother is right here."

Kira jumped. She recognized the ice in that voice.

"Hey, Mom," she said casually, turning around with a weak smile.

The eyebrow raised and Kira's spirits dropped. So it was going to be a lecture. *What is the point of narrowly escaping death*, Kira thought, *if you still get yelled at by your mother?*

"We're leaving." She grabbed Kira's hand. "Good to see you, Luke."

"You too, Mrs. Dawson," he said, looking at Kira like a deer caught in the headlights. "Um, is that my sister over there?" He waved to no one and slipped away quickly.

Coward, Kira accused with a grimace.

"Come on." Her mom tugged on her hand.

"But Grandpa, he said to go to the house, to reconvene, to talk strategy…"

The eyebrow rose higher.

"Your grandfather can wait," her mother said.

Kira took a deep breath, trying to think of a response, but the air just spilled out, completely deflating her body.

"Yes, Mom."

Chapter Three

"Get in the car." Her mother held open the passenger side door of the black town car she had arrived in—her eyes were daring Kira to refuse, to give her something to really yell about.

Kira slipped quietly under her arm, trying to keep the fight at bay for as long as possible.

Her mother slammed the door and walked quickly around to the driver's seat. When it banged shut, Kira's heart jumped. The only noise filling the car was the engine revving to life. Her palms began to sweat, and she rubbed them against her legs.

From the rearview mirror, to her mother's white knuckles, to her own twiddling thumbs, Kira didn't know where to look. Her gaze shifted, moving more frantically the longer her mom remained quiet. It was the calm before the storm—the moment when you knew disaster was coming and there was nothing you could do to prevent it, no last minute plea.

They were on the main road, driving aimlessly through the streets of Sonnyville, moving slowly with no sense of direction. Kira realized her mother had no idea where to go. Her eyes were barely focused on the road, and Kira could see the wheels in her head spinning on overdrive. She was thinking about her lecture, about where to begin. And the fact that it was taking so long had Kira on edge—it meant she was about to yell at Kira...a lot.

Her mother's lips were white, sealed together in a tight line. Even knowing that it would open a floodgate, Kira couldn't stand to keep silent any longer. The anticipation was driving her insane. She leaned toward her mom, keeping her face open and innocent—trying to look like the wide-eyed child her mother loved and not the disreputable teenager she had become.

"Mom?" she whispered.

Her mother's hands shifted on the wheel, squeaking against the leather.

"I know you're mad—"

"Mad!" Her mother turned, taking her eyes completely off the road. "I'm furious! How could you?"

Dang, Kira thought, *why did you have to ask such an open-ended question?* Was she mad about Kira going to England, Tristan being a vampire, the Punishers bringing her to Sonnyville...the list could go on and on. Maybe if she stayed silent, her mother would just keep ranting…

"Well, Kira? What do you have to say for yourself?"

Kira looked around, desperately hoping something out the window would give her inspiration. At a total loss for words, she went to her classic fallback. "I love you," Kira said slowly, offering up her super wide "I'm sorry" smile.

"Oh don't give me that—that face stopped working when you hit puberty. I mean, how did you even get a passport?"

Ah, England it is, Kira thought.

"Mom, I never wanted to lie—it was just, I needed to go to see if my birth mother was alive, to see if I could save her." She wasn't listening, Kira realized as her mom continued mumbling.

"And Tristan is a vampire? How could you not tell me?"

"Well, I mean, I thought you would figure it out. You are a Punisher."

"And you've killed people?"

"Only vampires—"

"And you let them drink from you?"

"Not from me, jeez, there were other factors—"

"And you've been lying to your father and me for months, not even trying to include us."

"In what? In my life as a conduit? You didn't exactly want to be included, Mom. You could have asked me about it. You could have checked in once in a while—why is that all on me?" Kira shifted in her seat, staring at her mother, trying to gather some strength. This was not all her fault.

"You didn't tell me about your powers, about how strong you are."

"All you had to do was sit in on one training session with Luke—just one and you would have known about my abilities. You're the one who asked me not to tell Dad, to leave him and Chloe out of it. You pushed me away. You edged me out of the family."

Her mom refused to look at Kira but stared straight ahead. They were on the main drive, heading out of town. In five minutes they would be at the gate. Kira recognized this tree-filled street—she had sped down this road a few too many times before.

"I didn't push you away. I wanted you to have a normal life." Her mother's voice had softened slightly.

Under any other circumstance, Kira would have been amazed at her skills. Somehow she had turned this fight around and escaped a thrashing. But victory was the last thing on her mind. The two of them had danced around this fight for a long time. Kira had been keeping these feelings in for too long—she had opened a floodgate all right, but it was within her own heart and not her mother's.

"Well, I'm not normal, Mom, and neither are you. I'm strong and powerful, and it's part of me now. And you have to accept that."

"I won't accept it." Her mom pushed her foot down on the gas pedal a little more. "I won't accept you being in danger all the time and people arguing over the fate of your life. I won't accept my own people begging for your head."

"Please, your own people? You don't even know what being a conduit is. You don't understand."

"I understand that fighting for your life every second of every day is no way to live. I understand waiting at home for your family to come back from a mission, never knowing if they'll show up alive. I understand losing people. And I won't let that happen to you."

A tear rolled down her cheek and Kira realized her mom wasn't blinking. Her eyes were wide, staring straight ahead at something Kira couldn't see. Her entire body was stiff, unmoving.

Farther down the road, Kira saw the gate—a black shadow across the road growing bigger by the second. It was opening slowly, anticipating their approach.

"Mom, slow down. Where are we going?"

Her mother didn't move.

"You can't do this anymore, Kira. All the lies and all the fighting, I won't allow it." Her fingers trembled on the steering wheel.

"Okay, Mom," Kira said softly, putting a hand on her forearm. She had never seen her mother so out of control.

"I won't lose you like this, Kira. They're crazy."

"I know, Mom, vampires are out of control—"

"No." Her mom shook her head, keeping her eyes wide. Her pupils were so dilated with adrenaline that her eyes looked almost black except for a narrow sliver of yellow-green. "Not the vampires, Kira. *Them*. The conduits. I'm taking you away from these people. From their rules and traditions. I'm saving you."

Her eyes began to glaze over, filling with water as more tears dropped down unnoticed.

"Mom, they won't hurt me."

"They already have, Kira, don't you see. They pushed me away because I wasn't strong enough. They're the reason my brother is dead, because he didn't conform to their rules. And now you. They let you live just to change their minds years later? They're afraid of you, of anything new and different. And I won't let them have you." She shook her head back and forth.

"Mom." Kira gripped the steering wheel over her mother's hand, holding her cold fingers and trying to keep the car steady. "Mom, I'm safe. I'm right here with you. Nothing is going to happen to me."

The blood began to flow back into her mother's fingers.

"Mom, slow the car down."

She eased her foot off of the pedal. Kira shifted her weight over the gear stick, wrapping her arms around her mother's trembling torso.

"Shh, it's okay," she soothed.

The car slowed to a stop, and they rolled almost unperceptively through the gate. But the sun filled Kira's veins as they passed through the invisible UV barrier thrumming across the entrance, blocking vampires. The two of them were outside of Sonnyville, finally escaped from conduit lands, and it was enough for her mother to break. Heaving sobs filled the car and hands clutched Kira, gripping her tight and pulling her into her mom's body.

"Oh, Kira, I was so afraid," she cried.

"I'm alive, Mom. I'm not going anywhere," she said and ran her hands through her mother's hair, the same way her mother used to do for her when she was scared or upset.

"Every time I look at you, I see your father. In the way you laugh, in your open and loving smile, in the brightness shining from your eyes. You remind me so much of him," she said quietly, speaking just loud enough for Kira to hear. "I can't lose you too."

"Mom," Kira said, leaning back to meet her gaze. "I love you, and I'm not going to let anyone hurt me, conduit or vampire, I promise."

She nodded.

"Let's go back to my grandfather's house. We can get a cup of tea, talk about everything. I'll answer any questions you have about what I've been doing."

"That would be good." Her mother nodded again, and Kira eased back into the passenger seat, still holding onto her mom's warm hand. She put the car back into drive, pressing slowly down on the pedal to turn the car around.

"I love you," Kira said.

"I love—"

Metal crunched, screeching in protest as the door was ripped free from the moving car. White hands grabbed her mother's shoulder, wrenching her from her seat before she even had time to scream. Kira gripped her hand, holding onto her fingers for as long as she could before they were tugged hard and slipped free of Kira's hold.

"Mom!" Kira screamed.

Reaching for her seatbelt, Kira unbuckled and forced her door open. Without thinking, she dove out of the car, rolling on the ground and scraping against rough asphalt. Behind her, the car screeched, swerving wildly, and smacked into a tree. But Kira's eyes were on the forest.

"Mom!" she yelled, listening for any scream to tell her where to run. Bringing a flame to her palm, Kira sent her power out into the woods, hoping to hear a vampire squeal.

Silence.

The car door was still on the ground, left like a mangled toy. Kira rushed to the spot, looking for any sign of life. Under the ripped wires and torn metal was a spot of blood—fresh, red, and most definitely human.

Toward her left, Kira spotted another dark shadow in the grass, just beyond the edge of the road. More blood.

"Mom!"

Still no sound of life.

Kira pushed past the branches, walking off the road and into the trees, trying to spot another hint. Every leaf was green, every branch brown—the only red she saw was the berries on a few low bushes. Spinning in circles, Kira inspected every surface she could find, almost wishing for vampire-like scent.

"Kira!"

The scream tore through the woods, ringing in Kira's ear like a loud siren. In an instant, she was sprinting toward the sound.

"Kira!"

The shout was slightly quieter this time, as though a little bit of her mom's spirit had been taken away, a little bit of fight had been lost.

But it was enough of a sound for Kira to follow, and she kept running, pounding her feet through soft mud, pushing branches aside, letting sharp leaves scratch her cheeks. Until finally, Kira saw a little flicker of life through the darkness, a tiny spark shimmering through the leaves.

Her mother's flames.

They were small—a barely roaring fire, enough to warm but not to burn. Even from afar, Kira saw the mocking face of the vampire opposite her mother. Those flames wouldn't be enough—they already weren't enough. A trickle of blood streamed down her mom's neck, flowing slowly but fast enough to drain the life from her body.

"Hold on, Mom!"

Kira threw her fire out, shooting it as far as it could travel, barely licking the vampire's face. But Kira's fire wasn't like her mother's, and the smallest touch was enough to send the vamp to its knees. The closer she ran, the more it burned, until finally he exploded, turning to ash under the torrent of her strength.

Without pausing, Kira fell to her knees next to her mom.

"Are you all right?" she asked, cradling her mother's head in her lap and shooting her powers into the two little holes puncturing her neck.

"Kira—"

Hands grabbed Kira's throat, pulling hard on her spine and throwing her fragile body against the base of a tree. Hearing a crunch, Kira cried out in pain. Her body fell limp. Her fingers were lazy, unmoving, and her legs were like stone, unbendable and far too heavy to move. Like a doll dropped carelessly on the ground, she was contorted at inhuman angles.

Her mother's eyes widened and a scream curled on her lips. But before a sound could escape, another vampire jumped out, biting down on her throat and swallowing the yell along with her blood.

Kira tried to throw her flames, but her body needed to be healed and she turned her fire inward, searching along her spine for the fracture that culled her movement.

Sensing her shifted focus, the vampire looked up. Its blue eyes bored into Kira, searing her with their freeze.

"A note from Aldrich," he said, his voice low and his teeth stained with blood. "I took one mother from you, and I can easily take the second, along with any other person you love. Be warned."

He smiled and sank back down, reaching for the blood again. But Kira found the spot—the broken bone, the severed nerves—and sent her powers there. Sensation slowly extended back to her body, her nerves thrummed to life again sending tingles down her limbs.

Her mother was growing paler. Her eyes sealed shut and her head started to slip farther into the ground, growing heavy.

She's not going to make it, Kira thought. Her fingers twitched, gaining strength once more, but her arm was still too heavy to lift, too weak to let her aim her flames.

"Mom!" Kira yelled, knowing it was useless but needing to do something. Her memories flashed back to the same image—a blond woman still on the ground while vampires swarmed over her. All the sudden, Kira was the baby hiding under a bush, watching helplessly while her parents were stolen from her.

But now she could fight, and Kira refused to lose another mother the same way. She wouldn't.

Her mother's body went limp, but before Kira could respond, a white blur streaked across the trees, slamming into the feeding vampire. He flew back, rolling over in the dirt, and without a moment of hesitation, the white blur reached through the vampire's chest and tore the heart from his body.

Now still, Kira recognized their savior. The vampire's hair rolled down her back in long ebony waves, her skin had an olive glow, and her eyes were just slanted enough to be interesting. More than anything, her hip was cocked, giving off an air of defiance that Kira remembered very well.

"Pavia!" Her voice ringed with relief and excitement, something no vampire other than Tristan had ever been able to elicit from Kira.

"Sorry to crash the party, but I thought you could use a hand." She shrugged and kicked the dead vampire crumpled on the ground. "Aldrich's cronies," Pavia said with a note of disgust. She spat on the body by her feet.

Kira sat up slowly, stretching her strengthening limbs. "Thanks."

"Least I could do." Pavia walked over to her mom, inspecting the wound. "I technically killed your other mom, thought I could at least save this one. Talk about timing though. I can feel her life is almost gone, her blood is…" She sniffed the air, kneeling down a little. "Well, you don't understand, but her blood just smells like death."

"Can you bring me closer?" Kira asked. She tried to stand, but fell back down on rubbery legs. Pavia grabbed her under the arms, dragging her a few feet across the ground so

Kira could rest a hand on her mother's chest. Her flames flowed out, sinking deep into her mother's chest, and expanding effortlessly through the conduit body that welcomed her power.

A conduit. Kira had never really thought of her mom that way, but the sun flickered deep inside her mother's heart.

"So what's wrong with you?" Pavia nudged her foot, pointing out Kira's depleted strength.

"The vamp broke my back," Kira said, sending a shiver down the very spine she had just healed. It sounded worse when she said it out loud. Pavia winced.

"I've been there, definitely not pleasant."

"I'll be fine in a few minutes," Kira said, taking note of her mom's returning color. Her skin darkened to its natural bronze. Her heartbeat strengthened.

"Good, because there are more on the way. Maybe five?"

Her mom blinked.

"Kira?" she said, woozy and confused.

"It's okay, Mom, you're safe." Kira put a hand to her cheek, relieved with the warmth she found there.

Kira stood, finally feeling strong enough, and pulled her mother to her feet as well.

"Mom, I know you don't understand, but this is Pavia and she won't hurt you, okay?" Her mother nodded, still too out of it to really comprehend Kira's words. "Pavia," Kira said, switching her attention, "I need you to take my mom back to the gate. You won't be able to cross, but put her as close to the UV barrier as you can. I'll take care of these vampires, and I'll meet you soon."

Pavia nodded and scooped her mother up into her arms. "We have to talk later," she said. "Just you and me. I have a promise to fulfill."

"Just keep her safe," Kira said, showing her agreement. The promise was to show Kira more of her birth mother's memories—Kira hadn't forgotten about it, and she was relieved that Pavia hadn't either.

"They're almost here," Pavia said and then left, disappearing through the trees, leaving Kira to face the vampires alone. And she was ready for it. Feeling helpless was not her style, and already her flames danced down her wrists, flickering over the grass and sparking with excitement.

When the first vampire broke into the clearing, he burned within seconds. Her fire was spewing lava—no one could escape it.

The second fell just like the first, without any hesitation, without any real use of strength on Kira's part. They went down easy, like squishing a bug on the ground. She almost wanted more of a fight—it was too effortless to be satisfying, too effortless to be rewarding. As her flames grew stronger, so did her conviction, and Kira wanted it to hurt. After watching her mother come so close to death, someone had to pay.

A third vampire came in from the left side and a fourth from the right, trying to corner Kira by dividing her attention. She stretched her arms to the side, flinging her power in both directions, trapping each vampire inside of swirling flames.

Her fire licked their skin, teasing them with the heat, searing their flesh and then retreating again. One yelled out, growling a deep sound mixed with fear and anger. It was a caged animal, and Kira squeezed her fingers, letting the fire close in and slowly suffocate it. The vampire fell, bursting into dust, imploding from the inside out.

On her left, the other vampire started to panic. He pushed against the flames, trying to breakthrough but retreating when puffy boils sprouted along his arms.

Kira crushed him easily, still ready for more fight.

Then finally, the fifth and last vampire entered the clearing. His movements were slow, as though he had no fear. He confronted Kira openly, not trying to gain the element of surprise.

Almost curious, Kira pushed her fire out. Immediately she sensed something different from his body, and her power was met with resistance, almost like an invisible shell encased his torso.

Conduit blood, Kira thought at first, but this shell was different. It wasn't a bubble around him that could be popped—it was in him, part of him. But his hair was a ruddy brown, his eyes the cold, icy blue of a vampire. Suddenly, Kira realized that she had seen that hair before, on her younger sister. He must be a half-conduit, a mix of human and maybe Punisher, one that had been turned bad.

Kira switched her strength, testing her Protector flames, which sunk deeper into his skin, burning his marbled flesh to a bright red.

He kept coming closer, slowed by her powers but not stopped by them. Kira pushed further, letting a sliver of her killing Punisher powers seep out. Simmering with heat, they sunk in, creeping closer to his heart, forcing their way through every inch of his skin.

But he kept approaching, getting closer and closer to Kira's body, closer and closer to a place where he could attack.

His skin began to blacken and flake off where the Punisher flames took hold. His features hardened into a grimace as the pain of death took its toll and Kira smiled, pressing her advantage. Finally, someone was paying for what had happened to both of her mothers. His hurt was her strength. His fear was her drug. And as he crept closer, the emotions fed into Kira. Every wince made her feel empowered.

Then without her even realizing it, the blackness crept out of Kira's heart, flowing into her flames rather than pressing against them, and her fire darkened. The bright orange, yellow, and red flames became tainted. A river of black flew with them, encircling the vampire in a mix of fire and shadow. The hot lava flowing through her veins became slick and oily, a searing tar that bubbled with a heat that came not from lightness but from anger—a sea of cold fury that felt somehow hot enough to burn.

Her flames wavered.

The darkness pressed inward, suffocating her.

Kira's fire winked out, fading quickly away, and before she knew enough to fight, something else had taken over. Something that welcomed the shadows, the evil. Something that pushed her over the edge, made her fall, spiraling down, down, down.

The conduit was gone.

The vampire hiding underneath her skin took over.

Kira's eyes shot up, locking on the dying man before her. His fear pushed out in waves, and he retreated. Kira stepped forward, closing in on her prey.

And before she realized what she was doing, Kira pounced, sinking her teeth into his burning flesh.

Chapter Four

His blood was dark, not filled with enough light to satisfy, and Kira dropped his lifeless body to the ground. Against the rough dirt, his frame finally combusted, but Kira wasn't paying attention. Her nose was filled with the scent of the sun—a golden honey sweet enough to make her sigh.

She wanted to taste it.

So she ran, light on her feet, and almost flew through the forest, following the sugary trail of conduit blood, the small droplets that sang to her senses.

When she broke through the trees, Kira saw it—a body resting on the ground, glowing with the sun. A halo of gold sparks surrounded the figure and Kira sniffed, drunk on the elixir running through those veins.

Without thinking, she ran and dove for the woman.

And then she burned, screaming out in pain as the sun assaulted her body, burning the vampire away, boiling the ebony oil in her veins until it evaporated in wisps of shadow that seeped out of her pores. Her every nerve was on fire. Pinpricks that felt like knives stabbed her limbs.

Kira curled onto her back, writhing in agony. The smell of honey still haunted her nose, but instead of a sugary sweetness, it was a searing iron, melting her insides as the fumes traveled downward.

But deeper down, the conduit praying for escape welcomed the pain, begged it to come in faster waves. Her flames were trapped—swirling in a sinking abyss, hoping the sun would come release them.

And when a burst of light finally broke through the darkness, Kira erupted.

The force of her conduit power returning lifted Kira off the ground, throwing her farther into the heat of the UV wall surrounding Sonnyville. Her hands lifted toward the sun, shooting long waves of flames into the sky. A current of light shot through her body, sending fire through every nerve and lighting Kira up from the inside out. Against the onslaught, the shadows retreated. The vampire left Kira's body in waves of smoke.

A minute later, Kira was on the ground, completely still, basking in the warmth of the sun and muddling through her returning consciousness.

She sat up, rubbing her sore head.

"Wha…?" Kira looked around. How did she get out of the forest? Was there another vampire after her?

Looking around, Kira spotted the body on the ground.

"Mom!"

She crawled over. Her mother was breathing deeply, but looked unharmed. Kira remembered healing her, remembered sending her back with Pavia, remembered fighting a few vampires.

Her mom blinked and sat up on her elbows, waking from a daze.

"Kira? What happened?"

"Nothing, Mom." Kira held her hand. "There were some vampires, but we got away. We're safe. I'll be right back."

She tried standing, took a few slow steps, and then crossed through the barrier again.

"Pavia?" Kira asked. Twirling around, she scanned the forest. Her nose picked up a strand of sugar passing on the breeze. What was that?

She followed the smell as it reeled her in. The mangled door was still on the ground. Drawn to it, Kira stopped a few inches from the torn metal. Why did it smell sweet?

And then she saw the pool of blood through the cracks in the windshield. Stumbling backward, Kira fell to the ground, landing painfully on her bottom as the memories flooded back.

She bit someone.

She bit a vampire.

Bit.

Tasted blood.

Kira started hyperventilating. Her entire body began to shake, a slow tremble that grew to a frantic pulse.

She had tried to bite her mother.

She had wanted conduit blood.

The blood still teased her senses.

Turning, Kira stared with wide eyes at the gate. The barrier, it had to have been what saved her. The UV light had burned the darkness from her skin—she vividly remembered the pain.

But part of the vampire was still lodged inside of her, was still drawn to the conduit blood spotting the ground, still pulled in by its sweet scent.

Iron melted in her mouth, sticking to her dry tongue, and she flipped over to spit out the vomit curling in her stomach. It came out red.

Kira scrambled away, ripping her palms on the rough concrete as she struggled to escape. Her back sank into the UV wall and Kira collapsed, letting the sun sink into her pounding head. Tears fell in long streams and she rolled to the side, pulling her legs into her chest, letting the shakes wrack her figure.

"I bit someone, I bit someone," Kira said over and over again, a low whisper that was too soft for even her ears to hear.

"Kira!"

She didn't register her name.

"Kira!"

Again, the words were lost to her.

"I've been saying her name for five minutes," a woman's voice called from a few feet away.

"Kira!"

Hands grabbed her shoulders, rolling her over, but Kira's eyes were wide and full of water. The world was a mix of brush strokes that didn't make sense to her overloaded brain.

"Kira, it's Mom, what's wrong?"

She didn't move.

"What happened?"

A deeper voice asked from over Kira's shoulder.

She heard the words around her, but didn't understand them. Her mind had turned red—she was drowning in the blood settling in her stomach.

A fissure broke through, cracking along her brain, forcing foreign thoughts into her frozen senses. They were white and airy, flecked with yellow. Like balloons, they floated higher, forging a path through the crimson droplets raining down on her.

Kira's mind started to settle. The tremble in her body slowed and a sense of peace settled over her—a borrowed sense of peace.

"I think it's working," a low voice said.

"Luke?" Kira whispered, aimlessly reaching out her hand, striking gold as her fingers brushed his warm skin. A hand clutched hers, trapping her fingers in a worried grip.

"I'm right here, Kira."

Trusting those words, she blinked and his face, silhouetted in a halo of gold, smiled down on her. Kira pulled up, or maybe Luke reached down, but within seconds she was wrapped in his sturdy arms, letting her cries disappear into the soft cotton of his T-shirt. His hand ran soothingly through her curls and he rubbed small circles into her back. He whispered soft, secret words into her ear, stilling the chills running down her spine.

"Kira, what happened?" he asked after a few minutes, when he felt her heartbeat return to normal.

Kira shook her head against his chest. "I can't."

"Kir—"

"I can't!" she shouted, jumping out of his arms to pace across the street. She didn't want to think of it ever again. She refused to acknowledge the smell still tantalizing her senses, the new awareness of his warm pulse, the shadows dancing around her frightened heart. She refused to acknowledge that the hunger was still there, even as the UV wall penetrated her skin.

Luke cocked his head, trying to understand what was going on inside of her. Above him, with one hand on his shoulder, her mother stood, looking just as perplexed and concerned.

"Pavia," Kira said, abruptly changing the subject.

"Over here."

Kira turned. "Where were you?"

"Relax, I just took a quick look around. No more vampires, well, except me of course." She grinned and shrugged.

Kira breathed a sigh of relief, glad that the vampire hadn't witnessed the sun scorch her body.

"That guy mentioned Aldrich. He was here, waiting for me, because of Aldrich. What do you know?"

"I told you we needed to talk," Pavia said casually while sweeping her long hair back over to one side of her head, "but it can't be here."

"Fine." Kira spun on her heels. "Luke, we're leaving. Let's get Tristan and go."

"Are you serious?" her mom squealed.

"Deadly," Kira said. And it might be. She needed to get out—away from the Punishers, away from the conduits—before she went crazy.

"Kira, you can't just leave and run away all the time. What about the councils?" Her mother stepped forward, ready for the challenge. But Kira knew her real concern; she saw the panic settling in her mom's eyes, the deep-set fear running way back to her father's death.

"Mom, I can handle myself. And the Punisher Council doesn't even want me to speak. I need to end this— I need to find Aldrich, and I need to kill him. And," Kira paused, her eyes flicked over at Luke, "and I need to take Tristan home. There's nothing for me to do here."

"Kira, I forbid—"

"Mom, I know you're the parent, but I just saved your life and I think I deserve a little credit."

"She'll be fine," Luke said, putting his hand on her mom's shoulder reassuringly. "I would never let anything happen to her."

"But—"

"I swear," Luke said and squeezed her muscle, forcing her to relax.

Kira took it as her cue to press the advantage.

"Pavia, we'll be back soon," she called over her shoulder without bothering to look back. Her eyes were on the Jeep Luke had driven out to the front gate. In a few strides, she was at the door and jumping into the front seat. "So, how'd you know to come out here?"

Kira looked at Luke, who was buckling his seatbelt and putting the key into the ignition.

"Is that a joke? It looked like a bomb went off—your fire lit up the entire sky."

Kira squirmed in her seat, not responding to the question totally apparent in his words. Instead, she pressed the seat back, forcing it as flat as it would go and curled up on her side to stare out the window.

Her mother ran her fingers through Kira's hair, trying to calm her, and Kira stared unblinking at her changing surroundings, trying to still her trembling fingers. Luke sensed the mood and remained quiet, but Kira suspected the silence was more for her mother's benefit. As soon as they were alone he would burst, but what would she tell him?

That she had been pushed to the brink? That she had tasted...that she had almost fallen...had almost turned into a...that her powers had actually burned her? What could she tell him when she didn't even want to admit it to herself?

Kira emptied her mind, focusing on the wash of green flashing by the window. Trees were so much simpler to think about—trees and the bright cloudless sky and the vastness just outside her window, a place where she could disappear.

A chimney poked into her eyesight and Kira sat up, unsure of how much time had passed. They were in town, close to her grandfather's home.

"You guys explain it to the council," Kira said, her voice scratchy. "I'm going to sneak in to grab my things, and then I'll meet you at the hospital."

Luke looked over at her. Kira saw the movement from her peripheral vision, but was afraid she would break if she looked into his warm emerald and golden eyes. They were too familiar, too comforting, too willing to take away her fears. Instead, Luke reached across the seat and entwined their fingers. He pulled her hand over, touching his soft lips to the topside of her fingers, resting them there for a moment.

His fire swirled into her palm, warming her hands and traveling up to her heart, where it settled like a hot spring flooding into an arctic pool. A good shiver, a loving tremble, shot through Kira's body, and she leaned her head against the back of her seat, letting the tips of her lip curl up.

If her mother noticed Luke's more than friendly behavior, she stayed silent, letting the two of them have their moment. But it didn't last long, because Luke pulled the car to a stop and Kira reluctantly slipped free, leaving the car to put her plan into action.

First stop? Getting her locket back.

Kira circled the house until she reached the trellis next to the backdoor. Her grandparent's bedroom was only one short story above her head, and Kira knew her locket was in there. The day before, she had watched her grandmother wrap it in a silk handkerchief and place it lovingly in her jewelry box.

But that's not where it belonged.

It belonged around Kira's neck, with her father's wedding ring and the sun charm Luke had given her as a gift. Her three most valued possessions in life needed to be kept together, safe and close to her heart.

Kira stepped forward, reaching through the vines to grasp the slightly soggy wood that she hoped would remain standing long enough for her to scale the wall and get back down. She couldn't be seen—she couldn't face the council right now knowing everything she said would be a lie.

Kira lifted her foot, stepping sideways on the frame, propelling her body weight off the ground. Using it like a ladder, Kira continued creeping up the wall until her fingers brushed against a whitewashed window frame.

Sticking her hand up a little farther, Kira breathed a sigh of relief—it was open. She knew they slept with the window open, that they liked the fresh air and the sound of birds in the morning, but still, Kira was satisfied—something was finally going right.

As she pushed up, throwing the upper half of her body into the house, her senses jumped. A waft of sugar tantalized her nostrils, sending a hunger into the pit of her stomach, an ache that only knew one cure.

Kira pinched her nose, cutting off her sense of smell, and gasped, using her mouth to breathe. The house smelled overwhelmingly like conduits, like their blood—a forbidden fruit Kira just wanted to taste. She could almost feel the power of the council below her feet thrum through her body, a syrupy elixir.

The wooden walls of the suburban home were a Pandora's box in disguise, teasing Kira to just let go, to let herself fall.

She made a gas mask out of her fingers, cupping her lips so as little air as possible seeped into her system.

She needed her locket and then she needed out.

Stumbling to the bedside table, Kira threw the top of the jewelry box open with one hand while she kept the other one pinched around her nose. The locket was easy to spot, and Kira pulled it free of her grandmother's handkerchief, stuffing it in the pocket of her jeans.

With no time wasted, Kira fell back through the door, gulping down fresh air. Her lungs burned in a good way, a human way.

She sucked in a breath, holding it while she retreated into the bedroom to climb out feet first. She landed on her knees, clutching the mud with her hands while her breath slowed. Sonnyville was not a haven anymore—it was a trap.

Sitting up slowly, Kira unclasped the chain around her neck and slipped the locket back down. It landed with a chink next to her father's ring, and Kira looked at the three little charms, resting side by side in the sunlight.

Time to find the missing piece—Tristan. Kira had no charm, no trinket to symbolize their past, but that didn't mean she was about to leave him behind. Instead, she took off at a run down the mostly empty streets, not pausing to say hello to any conduits she passed.

Kira didn't stop until she stumbled to a halt in front of the automatic doors of the hospital. She waited for half a second for the glass to slide open, and then took off at a sprint again, not letting her nose process any smell around her, not giving her brain enough time to register how many conduits were in the building.

Even with her speed, the scent of honey blood drifted into her senses, spurring her on even faster, pushing her toward the only human in the building.

Tristan jumped when she burst into his room.

"Kira!" he said, and then he relaxed with the recognition—something that warmed Kira's heart. A smile spread across his features, lighting up his face and making it glow with excitement.

"Tristan," Kira said breathily, trying to regain her composure after her run. She slammed her hands down in the bed, steadying herself, and a few papers rustled. Leaning closer, Kira noticed a pile of sketches on the bed.

A pile of sketches of her face.

Soft curls danced around her frame, hiding her eyes in shadows as a small smile played on her lips. In another, her eyes lit up, seeming to glow through the page. In another, her palm was raised with a small flame that she seemed to offer to the viewer.

Traveling up the bed, Kira saw graphite shavings lazily resting on the sheets, a pile of peeled pencils on Tristan's thigh, and a half-finished outline of her features below his fingers.

Those fingers.

The tips were blackened, a side effect of rubbing the pencil into the pages. It was almost too familiar—her breath stopped.

Kira stopped.

Everything except for her eyes, which kept rising higher—higher up his muscular chest to his Adam's apple stopped on a gulp and his lips halfway to a smile. Finally his brown eyes, which she almost expected to be blue again.

"Tristan?"

She leaned forward, hanging on the unspoken words dancing on his lips...

"I didn't mean to be forward," he said, stiff and formal, not her Tristan.

Kira's body deflated. For a moment, she had thought, maybe—but no. Better not to go there, not now. Better to hold onto some dreams, especially while the rest of her beliefs seemed to be crashing down around her.

"I don't mind," she said gently, sitting half on the bed, afraid to lean too close to him.

"I didn't know what to draw and you were so kind this morning. I thought maybe we were friends." He shrugged. A light pink blush gathered on his cheeks, innocent and so new to Kira.

"We are friends." She grabbed one of the sketches just to do something with the hands that felt fat in her lap. "And these are beautiful."

"Once I started, it felt almost natural, as though my fingers had remembered something my brain didn't." He looked down at the sketches, running his pointer finger along her graphite cheekbone. Kira felt the ghost of a touch on her cheek, a haunting memory. "This is not the first picture of you I've drawn, is it?"

Kira swallowed deeply. "No, it's not."

"I didn't think so."

He sat up, reaching his hand out, stopping an inch from her face. Kira held her breath. After a minute, his hand fell back down onto the bed—gravity stronger than whatever memory he was grasping for.

"Why is it that I don't remember?"

"I don't know," Kira whispered.

"I think I want to."

Kira sighed. "I know this must be so frustrating. But it will all work out. I promise you'll get used to this new life."

Tristan nodded. "I believe your words, but something, some instinct I cannot shut off wants me to go back, to retrieve what I've lost."

His fingers brushed over her palm and his eyes squinted, looking deep into hers, almost as if he could see her soul. A shiver traveled up her arm.

"Trist—"

"You ready?" Luke's voice called and Kira jumped off the hospital bed, looking for a body to go along with the words. The doorway was empty. Had she imagined it? For some reason, she felt guilty, like she had been doing something wrong. Was Luke the angel on her shoulder...or the devil?

"Over here, genius," he said and Kira spun toward the window. His blond head poked through the open frame.

"I knew that."

"Yeah, right." He grinned and pushed the window open even farther.

"Ready for what?" Tristan asked. He quickly shuffled the papers together, removing them from Luke's eyesight, viewing him with a slightly hostile stare.

Some things never change, Kira thought, feeling almost like herself for a minute.

"We're leaving," Kira said.

"Here." Luke tossed a pair of dark wash jeans and a plain black T-shirt on the bed.

"What are these?" Tristan asked, holding the T-shirt up like it was a rag.

"Clothes," Kira said gently, pointing at Luke's similar ensemble.

"That was pretty much your standard look, man," Luke said. "The ladies dug it."

"Dug?" Tristan asked, confused. Luke's grin widened.

"This is going to be fun," he said, looking slowly at Kira. A mischievous glint sparkled in his eye.

"Luke," she said sternly.

He gave her a little shove toward the window. "Why don't you act as look-out."

"I mean it," Kira warned.

"I'm just going to help the man get dressed," he said in a totally unconvincing voice and nudged her a little more.

"If he comes out with purple hair or something…" Kira trailed off to duck under the window.

"Would I do that?"

"Yes," Kira said under her breath as she jumped the last few feet to the ground.

"Now, Tristan," she heard Luke say, but stopped listening when her eyes caught a red mass in the distance.

The Punisher Council.

All seven of them.

Walking this way.

Walking into the hospital.

"Luke! We have to get out of here now!"

Chapter Five

Kira stilled her entire body, not daring to move even her finger. *Maybe they won't see me*, she thought—*be the wall, Kira, be the wall.* Brick wasn't so far from a strawberry blond head. Of course, she was wearing a bright, almost neon green shirt, so that wasn't helping.

The first Punisher ducked into the hospital, and then the second, now the third. The door was only a few yards from the window above Kira's head. How long before one of them noticed her—or reached Tristan's room? Because Kira had no doubt that was their destination, to poke and prod the newly human vampire.

Too bad I got here first, Kira mentally high-fived herself.

The fourth was in.

Kira moved her hand a few inches higher and knocked on the window, trying to urge Luke along without making a scene.

The fifth was in.

She was going to kill him, both of them—how long did it take for a guy to put on a pair of jeans, even if he had never seen them before. A button here, a zipper there...it wasn't that hard!

The sixth moved forward.

Kira eyed the final Punisher. It was the leader, the one with a massive chip on his shoulder, the one who maybe had it out for her...scratch that, definitely had it out for her. He took a step forward, putting his body halfway through the door, and Kira held her breath, waiting for the rest of him to disappear.

But Luke chose that moment to stick his head out the window and tell Kira, "We have company."

The Punisher whipped his head around, eyes boring down on Luke and Kira.

"What?" Kira asked, turning around, forgetting her camouflage now that their cover was blown.

"I locked the door," Luke said while jumping down from the window frame, "but it sounds like there are a few angry conduits on the other side of it."

The Punisher yelled toward them, closing in on them while numbers five and six walked back out of the hospital to see what the commotion was.

"There are a few angry conduits out here, too" Kira muttered and tugged on his arm. "Where's Tristan? We need to get out of here."

"On my way," Tristan said, and swung through the window, slipping his feet outward so he easily dropped to the ground without making a sound. Kira took in the dark jeans, the black T-shirt, the way his body moved fluidly like a jungle cat. *Not now*, she thought and pushed the memories back, *not when I need to be on my game.*

To their right, the Punishers were closing in. The leader had gathered his flames, ready to blow them into Kira's face. Normally, that wouldn't scare her, but something inside of her was screaming in fear, running from the burn. Part of her was afraid that the flames might actually sting.

"Let's go," she yelled, trying to ignore the shriek in her gut.

Luke ran in the opposite direction, motioning for them to follow. Tristan went next, and with one final look at the council that should have accepted her, Kira followed the two boys around the corner.

In seconds, they reached Luke's get-away car—an old black Jeep. Luke hopped into the front seat, but Tristan stopped dead in his tracks. Kira slammed into his back, knocking the air out of her lungs.

"Tristan, come on." Kira shoved him toward the door.

"What is this?" he asked, mystified and slightly awed.

"It's a car, like a modern day horse and carriage, but with metal and electricity and gas." Kira said, trying not to laugh at how ridiculous that sounded to her. Luke, of course, didn't bother to hide his amusement, and Tristan just looked more bewildered.

"Just get in," she said, opening the front seat for him. After he settled in, Kira jumped in the back and looked out the rear window at the Punishers still running their way.

Luke pushed on the gas, and Tristan practically jumped out of his seat, grabbing the handle bar above his head as though his life depended on it. Kira saw his knuckles turn whiter and whiter the farther down the road they moved. She reached through the seats and put a hand on his shoulder.

"It's okay." Kira squeezed. "You're perfectly safe."

"You know, statistically speaking, cars are actually really dangerous," Luke said. Kira death-stared him through the rearview mirror. "What? I speak the truth." He shrugged. "I'm just a really awesome driver."

Kira rolled her eyes. "The best," she deadpanned.

"Hey, I've survived many a car chase, thank you very much."

"I know. I was almost killed in one of those car chases."

"By vampires."

"By your driving."

"You were totally safe."

"Because I was tied to the bed of the truck."

"Completely my idea."

"You and I have very different memories of that night."

"Mine being the right one?"

Kira stared at him, trying not to laugh as he smiled super widely into the mirror, giving her that all too innocent look she knew very well. *Total stalemate*, Kira thought and bit down on her lip. Luke's eyes crinkled at the corners, and Kira knew she was about to win the unspoken contest.

Three.

His smile wobbled.

Two.

He swallowed a gulp.

One.

He sucked in air.

"You talk very fast," Tristan said slowly, cutting through both of their defenses. Luke let out a loud hoot and Kira broke down in giggles. Tristan turned his head to stare at them both, utterly perplexed by the scene around him.

Curling her feet into her chest, Kira looked out the window and tried to ease her laughter. But it wouldn't stop. The lightness in her chest just kept expanding the farther out of Sonnyville they traveled.

The air smelled a little less like delicious honey.

The Punishers were pushed to the back of her mind.

Her worries seemed lost to the wind.

"Where's Pavia?" Luke asked as they neared the gate. Kira shifted her attention to his face, moving her gaze away from the mangled car that reminded her too much of what had happened only an hour earlier.

"Just keep driving, she'll catch up."

There was still a pool of blood on the ground that Kira was afraid to be near, a memory she was trying her best to bury.

"May I ask where we are going?" Tristan questioned, finally easing his grip on the handle a little bit. His eyes were still wide as they looked at the countryside flashing past the window. Kira watched his childlike wonderment in the side mirror, looking away when he tried to meet her gaze.

"To Charleston," she said.

"In truth?" he asked, turning around to look at her. The dimples she loved dug into his cheek.

Kira smiled—she couldn't help it. His excitement was contagious. "Yup."

"For how long? I would love to visit my home."

"I don't know," Kira said, turning her attention out the window again. She didn't have the heart to tell him his home was gone. The plantation he used to live in was dust sprinkling the marshes, torn to ash from a fire during the Civil War.

"It might be a little different than you remember," Luke said. Kira wanted to kiss him for the gentleness in his voice.

"It will still be home." Tristan leaned back, resting his head. "This car," he stumbled over the word, "it is far more comfortable than a horse."

Luke cupped a hand around his mouth, trapping the bark that was about to escape. "I like you this way, Tristan. Who knew you were so funny?"

"I don't mean to be humorous," he said, looking at Luke strangely.

"That makes it so much better." Luke sighed, shaking his head happily.

"You are very odd."

"He gets that a lot," Kira said, meeting Luke's eye in the mirror and smiling warmly. *But he's my oddball,* Kira thought, liking the way that sounded.

All of a sudden, a huge screech ripped through the air, and Luke slammed on the brakes. The seatbelt dug into Kira's shoulder, and she yelped as the car sputtered to a stop. The smell of burnt rubber filled her nostrils.

"What the..." Kira trailed off, looking up. "Good driver my as—" She stopped at the sight of Pavia standing with arms crossed an inch in front of the car.

"That was a little close, you know," the vampire said and grinned, winking in the process. She strolled around the car, opening the door behind Luke. Kira shifted from the middle, moving to squat behind Tristan as Pavia settled in.

"This is going to be fun," the vampire said cheerfully, looking at the two boys in the front seat. "You must be Tristan." She winked at him and turned to Kira. "Nice work. He's just as cute as I remember, well, you remembered and I stole. A little tanner, maybe, but that comes with the humanity I guess." She reached out, brushing a finger along his cheek, as if to check if there was really human blood pumping under his skin.

Kira knew what she was really doing. She slapped Pavia's hand down. "Stop."

"I was just taking a peek," she whined. "Besides, I didn't see anything useful. He's all blocked up."

"What?" Kira asked, tilting her head.

"There's a wall dividing his memories, something that's stopping me from retrieving them...for now." She raised her eyebrows, accepting the challenge.

Kira opened her mouth to ask another question, but Luke interjected.

"The name's Luke, by the way." A hard edge had crept into his tone.

"Nice to meet you," Pavia said, extending her hand in his direction.

"I'd rather not," Luke said.

"I see Kira told you my little secret, no fun." She pouted, looking at Kira accusingly.

"Oh please," Kira said, not giving into Pavia's little charade. "Now that the introductions are over, let's get down to business. You said you had to tell me something, something to do with Aldrich?"

Tristan sucked in a breath instinctively, catching Kira's attention. But there was no real recognition in his features. Kira knew what her Tristan's face would look like at the mention of that man—hard, a mix of steel and ice.

Pavia sunk into her seat, getting comfortable. Her features softened as the mask fell and Kira recognized this girl—this was the girl who promised to come back to Kira, to share more of her mother's memories, to fight Aldrich at all costs. The vampire with a heart, that one hiding inside of Pavia's tough exterior.

The teasing banter was lost to whatever grave news she had come to bear. Kira eyed her, watching the vampire's gaze shift from side to side as she struggled to make a decision.

Finally, Pavia sighed. "I don't know where to begin."

"It's only been a few days, how much can there really be to tell?"

A dark laugh escaped her lips. "More than you know."

"Start with Aldrich," Luke interjected. "What's his plan?"

"Kira could probably tell you that part better than I can," Pavia said and Kira sucked in a breath. Did she know? Know about the darkness lurking inside of Kira's chest, the black hole Aldrich wanted to push her into—the one her body seemed almost willing to fall into?

But no, there was no secret hiding in Pavia's glance. She really didn't know what Aldrich wanted so badly, why he was chasing so forcefully after Kira.

"Besides," Pavia continued, "that's the end of the story. I guess we should start with him." She pointed at Tristan.

"What about him?" Kira asked. Protectiveness lurked in her tone, roughing it up.

"Are you kidding? From now on, everything is about him."

"Me?" Tristan asked, shrinking into his seat.

"I guess I should start with Aldrich escaping—which I'm still pretty impressed about by the way." She threw a pointed look in Kira's direction. "You seemed pretty dead set on killing him."

Kira shrugged, unable to meet Pavia or Luke's eyes. "Can't win them all."

"Well anyway, the man's got a serious grudge against you. He wanted to unite the vampire community, to give them something to fight about together, and Tristan became his rallying point. I mean, a vampire that became a human again? That's some scary stuff to a lot of vamps out there."

Tristan turned his gaze out the window, and Kira tried to read the expression gathering on his face, the far-off look in his eyes.

"Why scary?" Luke asked from the front seat.

Pavia fell back, thinking. "I'm not sure how to explain it, but it's like, when you're a vampire nothing really matters. Your actions don't have consequences, and you can do very bad things without feeling any real remorse about them,

Scorch

things that a human wouldn't do."

As Pavia spoke, Kira kept watching Tristan. He brought one hand up and over his eyes, using his thumb and middle finger to rub at his temples. He didn't want to think about any of the past he didn't remember. Kira couldn't imagine the ideas running through his head, the questions about the things he may have done.

"But Tristan doesn't remember," Kira mumbled.

"But none of us knew that, and a lot of vampires would do anything to ensure that they are never human again—that they never have to feel the weight of humanity run through their veins ever again."

"So they're after Kira now... well, again?" Luke asked—no ounce of surprise tainted his words. This was business as usual.

"Some, yeah, but not me—and not a group of vampires I've been talking to for the past few days."

"What do they want?" Luke asked roughly, the Protector in him coming out full force.

"Down boy," Pavia muttered, raising her eyebrows in Kira's direction. "They heard Aldrich's story, but it had the opposite effect. It excited them, energized them, gave them a new hope for something more. What they want, Luke, is their humanity back—what they want is to be human again."

"What are they willing to do for it?" Kira asked.

She clenched her fists. Her powers were in there, but Kira didn't know if they were up to the task, if Tristan had

81

maybe been a one-time thing.

"I'm sure we can negotiate something. Right now, all they want is to meet with you and to see that guy in the flesh." Pavia pointed at Tristan, who was still doing his best to tune out the conversation.

"Absolutely not," Kira said, her voice harsh and commanding. "I'm not taking Tristan there."

"I'll do it," he said softly from the front seat.

"No." Kira jumped in. "I want you to stay out of it."

"I need to help," Tristan said, louder this time. "I must do something."

"You will." Kira put her hand on his shoulder, squeezing softly. "I promise you will, but I can't let you do this."

"Kira," Luke interjected.

"No." She shook her head. "No, Pavia will just have to show them her memory of Tristan and that will have to be enough."

Pavia opened her mouth to speak, but then thought better of it. Kira was not in a negotiating mood, not when it came to Tristan. The last thing he needed was to be around vampires, to get more and more confused about what his life had been for the past hundred years. She wanted him to be safe, to settle into a normal human life—or as normal as it could be. Kira refused to save him just to put him in danger again. That was never going to happen, not on her watch.

"Luke and I will go, and that will have to be enough."

Pavia raised her hands in the air, as if to say she was giving up, and nodded. "They should all be on their way to Charleston—you are so predictable, Kira. I'll set something up once we get there."

"Good," Kira said, trying to warm her voice up a bit. She owed Pavia a lot, but man did that girl know how to get on someone's nerves.

"Conduits and vampires meeting in peace? To strategize together? This has got to be a first." Luke shook his head, his voice light with disbelief.

"That's not the only thing vamps and conduits can do together," Pavia said, her voice highly suggestive.

"Pavia," Kira said sternly. The uncaring vampire she didn't like very much was returning now that business talk was done.

"I was talking about car games. Get your mind out of the gutter, Kira," she said with a wink. "Although, I can see why thinking about Luke might send you there."

Kira looked away, willing the blush to stop before it reached her cheeks. Luke, always her savior, spoke up from the front seat.

"What car games did you have in mind? I'm pretty much the champion of the alphabet game."

"Oh please, there's no skill required in that game. How about twenty questions?"

"I'm down. Kira?" Luke asked. She nodded.

"Okay, me first," Luke said, taking control as an excited grin spread across his lips. "I've got it."

"Is it a place?" Pavia asked.

"Nope."

"A person?"

"Yup."

"Is this person alive?"

"Nope."

"Dead?"

"Nope."

"Something can't be neither alive nor dead, you are totally cheating," Pavia said.

"Look who's talking," Luke retorted.

"We are alive, thank you very much...but, are you thinking of a vampire?"

"Nope. And you're down to fifteen."

Kira smiled and looked out the window. She knew Luke too well and already knew what he was thinking about.

"Man?"

"Nope and fourteen."

"Okay, woman?"

"Yeah."

Kira smirked—she was totally right.

"Fictional character?" Kira asked and Luke met her eyes through the rearview mirror.

"Yeah," he said with a grin and Kira grinned back. Yup, Pavia would never get it.

"Does that count as one of my questions?"

"Nope, but that does. Twelve."

Pavia blew a bang from her forehead. Luke began to drum his fingers on the steering wheel—his victory was looking more and more imminent. Kira reached through the seats and turned on the radio. Car games weren't really her thing.

Instead, she settled in her seat and looked at Tristan, who was totally silent. His eyes were focused through the window, flicking back and forth with the trees flying by the car. But they looked lost.

For what felt like the first time she could remember, Kira didn't understand what was going through that pretty head of his. The wrinkles framing his frowning eyes were familiar, the purse to his lips was something she had seen before, and his straight determined nose was nothing new—but it was like a painting that had been replicated. Almost the same as the original but not quite. There was nothing specific Kira could pinpoint, but something intangible had changed.

She assumed he was thinking about his life as a vampire, what may have happened, but she didn't know the way she used to. Though Tristan had only been human for a few days, he had already started drifting away from her. And Kira wasn't sure if his memories would bring him back—if anything could bring him back.

His eyes moved in the side mirror, looking for hers.

Kira hesitated, holding his gaze for a minute, before looking away. A self-conscious bubble expanded in her chest, blocking her breath.

Maybe it was selfish, but she wanted to look into those eyes and see her Tristan again, just for a minute, to feel connected to him again. And Kira knew exactly how to do it. She just needed Pavia to play along once they got to Charleston.

When they got home, it would all work itself out.

"Only one question left!" Luke taunted, making his words come out as a song that caught Kira's attention.

Pavia looked annoyed and determined. She bit her bottom lip while she thought.

"Are you thinking about Catwoman?" she asked slowly.

"Nope! I win!" Luke started chanting from the front seat. His joy was contagious and Kira let it bubble up in her chest, flowing through their bond secretly. He really was like a drug, a little happy pill she could take whenever she wanted it.

"He's thinking of Wonder Woman," Kira told Pavia, fighting the grin that was widening her lips.

"Bingo! And that's why we're best friends," Luke said, and reached back to squeeze her knee.

Best friends or something else? Kira thought as the warmth from his hand traveled up her leg.

Charleston. Kira let the word keep her afloat. Maybe it was a pipe dream, but she had to believe an answer was coming soon.

Charleston.

Chapter Six

"Can you take a right up here?" Kira asked. They had been in the car for hours, taking shifts driving through the night, but finally they were almost home.

"Here?" Luke asked, confusion clouding his words.

"Just trust me."

He made the turn and continued driving until they reached the end of the road, which broke off right next to the Ashley River, a few miles away from Charleston City. He stopped the car and turned to her with an eyebrow raised.

"What are we doing here?"

"Tristan, Pavia—will you guys wait for me outside?" Kira asked, unbuckling her seatbelt to shift her attention to Luke. They were eye level, well almost, and both sitting in the front seats.

"You're not going to like this, but I have something to do before we go home and figure out the whole vampire meeting thing." His expression darkened, and a knowing look glazed over his eyes.

"You mean the whole keeping you alive and defeating Aldrich and changing the course of conduit history in the process thing?"

"When you put it like that, I see why this might annoy you, but it's just something I have to do."

Luke lifted his hand, rubbing the spot between his eyes. "Kira, I'm being patient and I'm giving you time, but I'm not just going to sit around while you try everything you can think of to bring your ex-boyfriend back—I'm just not."

Kira reached out, dropping her hand on his leg, trying to make him understand. "I'm not going to lie, I'm confused—about Tristan, about you, about myself—pretty much about everything. But I have to see if there is a way to bring his memories back, and it's not for me or about me. Can't you see how confused he is?"

"I do, I mean, I had to help the guy put on a pair of jeans." Luke laughed quietly. "The old Tristan would have probably slugged me for that. But, I'm being selfish this time, because I've been understanding for a long time. I thought that kiss meant you chose me, meant you wanted to be with me—"

"It did," Kira said, and at the time, it really did, but she had to resolve things with Tristan…a small part of her was still holding on, still refusing to let go, especially when he was so in need of a friend.

"Well, you have an interesting way of showing it."

He pulled the car into reverse and reached across the seats to open her door. But then she thought better of it. He paused, looking at her, vulnerable.

"Does he, I mean, can you...?" Luke trailed off, but Kira knew exactly what he was asking.

"No," she said quietly, "no, I don't feel his thoughts. I'm not sure why, but we're not connected that way."

The ghost of a smile crossed Luke's face, and then faded as questions flowed back into his mind.

"I'll grab some food. Let's meet back here in an hour," Luke said, his voice heavy. Kira stole one more look, keeping her mind locked tight so she didn't have to feel the pain coiling on his face, before stepping out of the car.

Without looking back, Luke made a U-turn and drove away. Kira kept watching the car until it disappeared down the end of the road—a big part of her heart went with it. He was right. Why was she holding onto the past when her future was right there, had been there all along keeping her happy and grounded and sane? What was she waiting for?

"Kira?" Tristan asked. "What are we doing?"

Kira spun on her heel. "Right. Sorry." She shook her head, clearing the fog Luke had created. "I'm taking you home—well, sort of."

"And what am I doing here?" Pavia asked. She had stepped closer to Tristan while Kira had been watching Luke, close enough to touch him.

"I need to borrow your expertise," Kira said, "but for now, follow me."

Only a few months before, a few months that seemed like a millennia, Kira had wondered the same thing—where was Tristan taking her? What was the secret place he was trying to show her? But now it was her turn to lead them off the road, through the low shrubs that lined the ground until they reached a marshy riverbank.

Kira kept walking, letting the two of them trail behind. Her memory was pulling her forward, was urging her up the river and against the current, until in the distance Kira spotted it—a low hanging tree branch that extended past the marshes, all the way until its branches licked the river.

Behind her, Tristan gasped.

Kira stopped moving.

Tristan sped past her, running toward the first place that seemed familiar to him since his reawakening.

Kira hardly noticed, a different more confident Tristan sprouted in her eyes—one that led her by the hand and kept looking back to see if she was all right, one that helped her hop onto the tree branch, one that looked at her with an almost hungry passion in his deep blue eyes. This was their spot to Kira, the place where he first told her all about his life as a vampire, the place where he first opened up, the place where their relationship really began.

But not anymore.

The new Tristan hadn't even looked back to see if Kira was still alive. He was speeding around the opening, running his fingers along the tree bark, marking this spot as his alone.

"Well, he's perked up, hasn't he?"

"Yeah," Kira said sadly. She didn't know why, but part of her had thought that bringing Tristan back here would make him remember. They had been here countless times together, from lazy Saturday afternoons in the spring to the midnight picnic he had prepared for their six-month anniversary.

Part of her had obviously been wrong.

"So what's the deal?" Pavia asked, nudging Kira with her shoulder.

"I want you to look into his mind, to see if there is a way you can make him remember." Kira didn't look at Pavia. Her eyes were still on Tristan as he climbed onto the overhanging limb and scooted out beyond the marsh to dip his feet in the water. He looked younger, like a little boy somehow.

Pavia eyed Kira, making a chill run down her spine.

"Is this for him or for you?" the vampire asked.

"I don't know," Kira said honestly, feeling better for finally letting the truth out.

"Fair enough." Pavia shrugged, pushing her sensitive side back undercover. "It'll be easier if I bite him."

Kira hesitated before nodding her approval. She

would do anything for an answer.

The two of them kept walking together, letting a silence settle over the clearing. Tristan had finally noticed them, had finally remembered he wasn't alone.

"How did you find this place?" he asked Kira, wonder etched into his words. "I used to play here as a boy. It was my secret oasis."

"You brought me here," Kira said softly, trying to hide the pain in her voice. He was gone.

"Really?" he asked, "I never even allowed my mother to follow me here."

"I know."

He settled his gaze on her, but Kira looked out at the river. She could feel his eyes as they traveled down and back up her body—she was a puzzle he was trying to figure out, a mystery he couldn't solve.

After a minute, he stood up on the branch and walked toward the trunk, jumping back down to solid ground. He took a step toward Kira, his eyes questioning, careful.

Pavia, who had been leaning against the bark, looked at Kira.

Kira nodded.

Pavia stepped forward and grabbed Tristan's hand, swinging him back toward her. In a flash, Pavia's teeth were diving for his neck, slamming into his veins before Tristan even had the chance to struggle. His body stopped moving when Pavia began to drink. His eyes glazed over and a silly smile spread across his lips.

Kira kept her eyes averted, hardly believing she was standing there doing nothing. Her fire itched her palms, scalding her muscles for their inactivity. A sucking, slurping noise sounded in her ears and Kira covered them, letting her flames seep into her skull, trying to drown out the sound with the crackle of her fire.

Tristan was being eaten, and she wasn't doing anything.

Her knees gave out, and Kira fell to the ground, still clutching her head.

A rock hit her shoulder and Kira spun, flinging her hands out.

Pavia jumped back with a yelp. "Watch it!"

"Sorry," Kira said, winking out her fire.

Tristan was a ball in the dirt. His eyes were closed as if in slumber, and Kira knelt beside him, cradling his head in her lap. She healed the two puncture wounds in his neck, sealing them closed.

"What'd you do?" she asked, her voice sad rather than accusatory.

"He won't remember being bitten. He'll think he fell from the tree."

"But what did you see?" Kira asked, looking at Pavia. Tristan stirred underneath her, shifting the head resting on her thighs.

Kira ran a hand down his cheek while his eyes flicked open, struggling to refocus.

"Are you okay?" Kira asked.

He nodded and sat up, clutching his head.

"Did I fall?"

"Don't worry, we won't tell anyone," Pavia said with a grin. He looked to Kira to confirm.

"Yeah, but don't worry about it," Kira said and stood up, brushing the dirt off of her legs. "Happens to the best of us." She offered her hand, yanking him to his feet.

He rose, his body a few inches from her own. Kira looked up, holding her breath at his proximity. Tristan lifted his hand, reaching in her hair. He shifted, running his fingers through her curls. Kira held back a sigh, but couldn't step away.

He pulled a leaf out of her hair and let it fall to the ground.

"Whoops," Kira said, finally moving away from the warmth of his body to feel for more leaves, but Tristan had found the only one.

He grabbed her hand to keep her from moving any farther away.

"I feel as though I know you, as though this has happened before," he whispered, "like maybe I have lived it once before in a dream."

Or a nightmare, Kira thought and snapped her hand out of his, moving a few feet away. He was haunting her, like a phantom of what had been. But Kira needed to wake up. This wasn't Tristan, not yet, and she needed to keep her distance. "What else do you want to see before we head back?"

"Is my house...?" He trailed off when Kira shook her head. No, his house was long gone. Tristan nodded. "Then I will just check one more spot, alone, if you do not mind." Kira nodded and he walked away from them, vanishing around the curves of a few large oaks.

"What'd you see?" Kira asked without turning around.

"His memories are all there," Pavia said slowly, walking into Kira's line of vision.

"So why doesn't he remember?"

"His humanity is like a wall, blocking them," Pavia said, stepping forward until she was close enough that Kira couldn't ignore her. "Do you remember what I said? Those other vampires are after you because this is exactly what they're afraid of. The human Tristan can't bear to remember what the vampire Tristan did, it would break him."

"So you can't bring them back? Not even one?"

"Not even one little memory of you?" Pavia asked, looking down at Kira with a knowing smile. "I could show him one of your memories, but his are an all or nothing deal right now. Bring one back and all of the others will follow. And I don't know what he told you, but there are some pretty dark things hidden in that very cute head of his."

"Don't," Kira said, fighting the urge to smack Pavia

across the cheek. The vampire was here to help, she tried to remind herself, here because they had a friendship of sorts.

"I'm just trying to make you understand," Pavia said, stepping back.

"I know." Kira turned to Pavia, ready with an apology.

Pavia held her hand up and shrugged. "As far as I'm concerned, we're good as long as those flames in your hands don't come shooting in my direction. I came back to help you, hard as it may be to believe."

"Because I saved you from Aldrich?"

"Because you gave me some hope," Pavia said, trailing off.

Kira looked at her, really took the time to take in the vampire standing in front of her. Aside from Tristan, Pavia was the only vampire she had met who seemed to want something more, who was tired of the shadow of immortality.

"Let's not hug this out, okay?" Pavia grinned, teasing.

"Deal." Kira smiled. "But can I ask you one more thing?"

Pavia nodded.

"What would you want, if you were Tristan?"

"I," Pavia started, but at that exact moment, Tristan reappeared, holding a mud-crusted box in his arms.

"I can't believe I found this!" he exclaimed, excitement coloring his words. Kira turned toward him, lighting her features with a mock enthusiasm.

"What is it?" she asked, looking away from Pavia, whose mouth was still hanging open, offering the answer Kira either dreaded or wanted to hear. There would be time to find out which later.

"A box I buried before the war." He knelt down in the grass and gently lifted the lid. "These were my prized possessions."

Lifting a small canvas bag, Tristan flipped it over in his hands and a handful of glass marbles dropped out. He rolled them around his palm, laughter dancing across his features.

"Marbles?" Kira asked.

"Glass marbles," Tristan corrected. "The best gift my father ever gave me."

"What else?" Kira asked, kneeling next to him. Why had Tristan never shown her these things before?

He took a cloth out and slowly unwrapped it like a present. A giant golden amulet gleamed in the sun, and Tristan picked it up by its gold-link chain. As it spun with the wind, Kira realized it was a pocket watch, still preserved incredibly well despite the passage of time.

Tristan put the device against his ear, slacking when he failed to hear it tick.

"Don't worry," Kira said and placed a hand on his shoulder. "I'm sure we can get it fixed somewhere."

He shook his head. "It stopped working the day my

brother died, the day I joined the army. I did not really expect to hear anything."

"Your brother died before you joined?" Kira asked. "I thought you joined together."

"No," Tristan said softly. "I did not start fighting until his death gave me cause to go to war. I enlisted with him out of duty, but eventually joined the war for him, despite all of our differences."

He set the watch back down and pulled out a third pouch. Kira sat back, stunned. Who was this man in front of her?

"My mother," Tristan said, revealing his final trinket, which was an elegant cameo of a woman's profile cut into rose quartz. "I'm surprised this is still here, I thought I would have come back for it."

"That's beautiful," Pavia said, leaning over Tristan's shoulder, running a finger over the pendant. "Before I turned, I used to dream of having jewelry like that."

"It was her wedding present from my father." Tristan folded the cloth back over the jewel, covering it up again. "It was meant to be passed down to my bride and to our children after that."

Kira tried to fight the sting of those words. Was she being an idiot? Tristan loved her, more than she knew a person could love someone else, but why had he kept these things from her? Why had his human life remained so far apart from the stories he told her?

"What's in the last pouch?" she asked, indicating the last unwrapped box.

"My paints," he said sadly, "but I doubt they've passed the test of time. I will open them later."

He closed the lid, shutting his personal side off. Standing, Tristan brushed the dirt from his clothes and swallowed deeply.

"I've seen everything I needed to see."

"Let's find Luke then," Kira said while stretching her body back upright, "he's probably back by now."

"Let's go," Pavia chirped and started walking. Tristan followed, and Kira brought up the rear.

As they reached the river, Kira took one look back. She would never be here again, and that was a promise. It had been a mistake to come, Kira realized. Whereas before, this had been their place, their oasis, Kira now felt like an intruder. It was Tristan's spot and it had been for years—Kira was just a blip on the radar, drifting farther away, getting quieter and quieter.

She knew what she had to do.

Tristan could never remember.

The first time they had met—five seconds before English class began, a moment Kira would remember forever—she had seen it then. The weight of time in his eyes, the heaviness over his heart. The more she grew to love him, the more she had seen why.

Life with Aldrich, watching everyone he had ever met

die, feeding off of humans to survive—it had been a burden on his soul. And she wouldn't be the one to bring that shadow back around him.

A few days ago, Kira had been ready to say goodbye to the vampire, but now she was ready to say goodbye to the man that had been inside of Tristan all along.

But there was one thing left to do.

One more burden to overcome before Kira could let him go.

Aldrich.

When the three of them finally reached the clearing, Luke was there waiting, as he always had been. He looked up over the rim of the sandwich he was biting into, and his eyes instantly traveled to the berth of space between Kira and Tristan. His shoulder slackened, the worry eased from his body.

But that wasn't what Kira wanted either. She didn't want Luke to feel like the leftovers. For once, Kira wished he could step inside of her head, to feel the way her pulse was quickening at the sight of him, to feel the peace that settled in her body just by thinking about him.

He wasn't second place.

He was the grand prize—the one hiding in plain sight this entire time.

So Kira opened the door and gripped the hand resting in his lap, holding on securely and letting warmth funnel through their bond.

"How'd it go?" he asked and rubbed his thumb along the sensitive skin of her palm.

"I know what to do," Kira said, looking into his eyes.

"And the rest of us are starving," Pavia sighed from the backseat. "Got any blood in that shopping bag?"

"Sorry." He grinned. "I'm a human-only lunch service. Tristan, turkey or ham? Take your pick." He tossed the bag of sandwiches into Tristan's lap.

Perplexed, Tristan pulled a ball of paper from the bag and began to unwrap it.

"Don't worry. It tastes really great." Kira smiled at him.

"Especially if you put some of those hot peppers on it," Luke suggested, eyeing the peppers spilling from his own concoction. "If there are any left."

"There better be some left!" Kira grabbed the bag. "I'm the one who introduced you to those things."

"And then the student became the master," Luke teased and took a huge bite from his sandwich, barely able to close his mouth without letting breadcrumbs slip out.

"Ah," Kira gave a satisfied sigh as she pulled a hidden plastic cup full of peppers from the bag. She opened the bread roll and dropped some on top of the ham and cheese before taking her own huge bite.

"So where to?" Luke asked when he was finally able to swallow.

Kira tried to respond, but ended up spewing bits of

her sandwich in the process.

"You are bringing it right now," Luke joked, wiping a breadcrumb from her cheek. He kept his palm there for a moment, cupping her face long enough to run his thumb along her skin. Disbelief channeled through Kira's mind, a satisfied disbelief. And Kira could read what it meant in his emerald green eyes, now alive with swirling flames.

Mine, Luke was thinking, finally she's all mine.

And Kira didn't look away.

The heat in his palm warmed more than just her cheek.

"I need to meet up with my gang," Pavia said from the back, blowing her bangs from her face in the process, "and I need to find a meal."

"Good, we'll drop you off downtown," Luke said, turning his attention back to the car and revving it to life.

"And then we'll meet up tonight," Kira demanded. There was no give in her voice. "You, me, Luke, and the vampires. If we're bringing Aldrich down, there's no time to waste."

"Agreed," Luke said.

"Done," Pavia confirmed.

Kira turned on the radio and leaned back, putting her feet up on the dashboard before taking another satisfying bite of her sandwich.

Aldrich was going down, and there was no way she would let him escape again—no way.

And, Kira thought, taking a look at Tristan in her peripheral vision, maybe he wouldn't have to be alone. If some of these vampires wanted to turn, wanted to reawaken to a new world and experience it with him, Kira would find a way.

No shadow in her heart, black as it was, would stop her.

Chapter Seven

"Spill," Kira said, eyeing Luke from the passenger seat of the car. Ever since they had left his house, Luke had been silent—never a good sign.

"Nothing." He shrugged.

Kira rolled her eyes.

Tristan was safe back in Luke's home, and Pavia was waiting for them at the meeting place, so Kira wasn't about to let Luke hide from her—not when it was just the two of them, alone for what seemed like the first time in ages.

"Luke?"

"Yes…"

"Luke," she pressed further.

He hesitated for a second before letting a huge exhale slump his shoulders. "Fine, fine."

Kira waited while he thought then poked him when she got impatient.

"It's just, we've done some crazy things—facing Diana, hiding out at the Red Rose Ball, taking Aldrich on at his home turf—but this seems a little insane. We're walking into a meeting with vampires, one where they'll definitely outnumber us and have the advantage."

"Is that it?" Kira asked.

"Well, yeah, mortal peril seems like a good reason to be a little wary."

"Mortal peril, really? I didn't know you were so chicken." Kira grinned, chiding him.

"Chicken?" He raised his eyebrows. "I'm best friends with you, that alone makes me braver than the little toaster, and he had the word brave in his name."

"Braver than a kitchen appliance…definitely something to be proud of."

"Did you ever see that movie?" He turned to her in disbelief. Kira shook her head. He tsked, "I'm disappointed."

"Ooh." Kira held a hand over her heart pretending to be wounded. "But really, back to topic, why are you nervous?"

"I guess…" He sighed. "Well, the only person who told us it would be safe is Pavia, and I just don't trust her. If you set this thing up, no questions asked, but something about her… I don't know, I don't like it."

"I trust her, isn't that enough?"

"But why? Why are you so sure?"

"You weren't there, but," Kira said, thinking back to the dungeon, to the hungry look for freedom in Pavia's eyes and the earnestness in her expression when she promised to show Kira more of her birth mother's memories. "It's hard to explain, I just trust her. She didn't have to come back, she could have run away from me and from Aldrich, leaving everything behind, but she didn't. She kept her promise. That's worth something, isn't it?"

Luke shrugged, still uneasy despite her reassuring words. "I just don't trust vampires."

"But you trust me."

"Always."

"Enemy of your enemy is your friend—these vampires want to get rid of Aldrich, we want to get rid of Aldrich. Everything will be fine."

"I hope you're right."

"Am I ever wrong?"

"Do you really want me to answer that?" Luke grinned, looking away from the road to meet her gaze for a quick instant.

Kira shoved him gently. "Just drive," she chided, but a giddy excitement stirred in her stomach.

"Where are we going anyway? This place is in the heart of Charleston."

Kira shrugged. "Pavia just gave me an address. She didn't say what it was."

"That's reassuring," Luke said wryly.

One hundred twelve North Market Street, Kira read quietly to herself. It was right in the historic district—what could it be? Someone's house?

Whatever it was, they would be there soon. Luke exited the main highway as they crossed over a large bridge into Charleston City. A few minutes later, he pulled to a stop next to a meter and stepped out of the car.

"Follow me," Luke said, turning toward the left and walking quickly down the street.

People were everywhere, relaxing outside of the ice cream shop and walking through the market place even though the street vendors had closed their stores. Couples held hands while they approached restaurants, and little kids ran around, ignoring the calls of their parents.

Where are we going? Kira wondered. This seemed like the least vampire-y place in the entire city.

Luke stopped.

"The Peninsula Grill?"

"What?" Kira asked, not understanding. Luke pointed to the sign hanging from a wrought iron fence. "Oh, it's the name of the restaurant. I get the hint, we can eat here sometime, but let's get to the meeting place."

"Kira, this is the meeting place. One hundred twelve North Market, right?"

She nodded and looked closer.

The entrance to the restaurant was a wrought iron fence that opened to a brick courtyard. The bushes lining the walkway were lit up with white Christmas lights, even though it was summer time.

"Here?" Kira asked.

Luke shrugged and stepped forward warily. They walked down the well-lit path for about fifteen feet before reaching the door to the restaurant. Luke stepped in first and Kira followed, but they were immediately stopped by a hostess.

"Good evening," she said, taking in their relaxed attire. "Do you have a reservation?"

"Um," Kira said, looking around for Pavia.

"Yes, Pavia? There should be a party waiting," Luke chimed in.

"Ah yes, in the private room. Follow me, please."

She stepped out from behind the podium, and Kira fought to keep up with her speedy steps. The entire restaurant was low-lit with candlelight, and crisp white linens topped the tables. Paintings hung from the cream walls and almost every diner sparkled with diamonds.

Kira thought of her jeans. Yeah, she and Luke weren't exactly the right clientele.

"Right in here," the hostess said and slipped a hidden door open, leading to a long table completely full aside from two empty seats on the opposite side of the room.

"Kira, Luke," Pavia said, standing and shooing the hostess away, "so glad you made it."

Kira was too distracted by the pale faces around her

to answer. Maybe Luke had been right...they were completely outnumbered.

"Sit, sit," Pavia continued, pointing toward the two open seats. Kira noticed that two plates of food were waiting for them—the only two plates of food on the entire table. In fact, the only other things on the table were ten glasses of red wine, or what Kira was pretending was red wine. But when she sat down and smelled what had to be filet mignon on top of a bed of rosemary mashed potatoes, she tried to calm down.

Luke, however, eagerly grabbed his fork, completely ready to dig in. So much for his concern.

"So, thank you all for coming." Pavia was still standing at the head of the table, looking around at all of her guests. Her formality was making Kira slightly uncomfortable—what was she nervous about? "You all know why we're here, because of her." Pavia pointed at Kira, and every head turned. "Because Kira has restored a vampire's humanity, and she says she can do it again."

"For the price of one war," the hawk-nose male vampire three seats away from Kira said.

"Alessandro, really." Pavia brushed him off, her blasé attitude returning. "It'll be one battle that we'll win without breaking a sweat. I've heard Aldrich's looking a little crispy lately, if you know what I mean."

The vampires snickered. Kira and Luke looked at each other and shrugged. Crispy?

"His power was of the mind, not the body," Hawk-Nose pressed again.

"Before we get to that part, I want to see some proof," a female vampire spoke from opposite Hawk-Nose.

"I would as well," another vampire farther away from Kira seconded. "Was she not supposed to bring Tristan?"

"Change of plans," Pavia said, moving back to her seat on the other side of Kira. "Will everyone join hands so I can share the memory with all of you at the same time? And before you ask, no, I can't see into multiple minds at once so you'll all block each other out."

Kira grabbed Luke's outstretched hand, watching as he winced and took the strong grip of the female vampire sitting next to him. She braced herself. This wasn't the first time Kira had seen a memory from Pavia and getting sucked into someone's mind wasn't exactly a pleasant experience.

Turning to her left, Kira looked Pavia in the eye. There was something fragile in her stare, something vulnerable that she probably didn't want Kira to see.

"This is a memory of my own," Pavia said, stopping her hand an inch above Kira's, "from the night that Tristan turned."

Opening her eyes in surprise, Kira tried to speak, but it was too late. Pavia's fingers touched Kira, and she was falling. Her chair tipped backward, sending her into a spinning vortex, an endless hole. Her feet seemed to flip over her head, colors swirled in her mind, noises racked her ears, but none of it was decipherable. Until the pull of gravity nudged her and she slammed back to earth in a body not her own...

She was running, faster than she had run in fifty years, farther than the tiny space that horrible glass shell had allowed. She felt free, freer than she maybe ever had before. Captivity was soul crushing, and the weight had been lifted from her shoulders. She felt as though she could fly, as though her feet, already pumping at an inhuman speed, would eventually lift free of the ground and propel her forward based on will alone.

The house was disappearing behind her, glowing from flames dancing through the windows, hopefully engulfing Aldrich whole.

That evil man.

He would pay, he was paying, even if it wasn't her revenge, the idea was still sweet on her lips. A sugary flavor making her hunger grow.

She needed to find a human. Now.

Refusing to stop running, she peered through the dark air, hoping for a lick of light to guide her way toward a house, but the landscape was quiet except for the flames still crackling in her ears.

But she wouldn't go back there. Not ever. Not for anyone.

The conduits had set her free and had let her go, a double escape, one she couldn't tempt. Not even for—

A scream pierced the night.

She stopped.

She recognized that scream.

Kira.

Kira screaming as though her life was being ripped from her body, which meant one thing—Aldrich was escaping.

Hesitating for a second, she spun on her heels. Aldrich had to pay.

The house was almost dark, smelling of burnt flesh and sunlight and a sweet delicious blood that teased her. She let her senses pull her onward, since the fire from before had died out. The fire she had been sure Aldrich would burn in.

As the house enlarged, she slowed down. She could smell them, the conduits all still in the house, waiting for instruction. But still, they were all still, so Kira couldn't be dying. But she was whimpering, her cries sounded softly through the night.

There was a window up ahead.

She moved quietly closer, hiding in the darkness she had missed, peering through the house toward the commotion.

There was Kira. She was kneeling on the ground, her hand stopped above a body of charred flesh, tears streaking down her face as her eyes grew wider and wider.

Aldrich. It had to be.

But what was Kira doing? Was she prolonging the kill? Do it. Faster. Just make sure he's gone.

And then flames appeared from Kira's palm, sinking slowly into the flaking burnt skin of the vampire at her knees.

Go, go, she thought, urging Kira on with her silent prayers. It would be a slow death, a painful one just like he deserved. His skin was darkening, melting off, sinking to the ground, but wait. What?

His hand.

She stared at his hand. Could it be?

The skin was flaking off. Burnt petals fell to the ground, landing in dust. But in their place was pink flesh, new, unscarred, unbroken, and thrumming with life.

Kill him, *she wanted to scream. But the bright fresh skin spread farther, up his arm, from his toes to his thigh, revealing naked, baby-silk skin. Until finally his face appeared—chiseled cheekbones that led to inviting lips almost smirked in a smile. He was beautiful.*

He was most definitely not Aldrich.

Hair grew from his scalp, black as night, framing eyes that remained closed.

Closed.

Until he sat up, opening new eyes, new brown eyes, or old maybe.

And then she fell back, back, back…

Kira jerked in her chair, almost expecting to land against the cold dirt of the English countryside. Pavia had come back that night? She wanted Aldrich dead so much that she returned to finish the job herself? And maybe, just maybe, part of her had come back to make sure Kira was still alive, that Aldrich hadn't won.

But she had called Tristan beautiful, and what was that feeling that came with her thoughts, something almost warm despite the cold nature of her body.

A fist twisted in Kira's stomach. What—

"So now you've seen it," Pavia said weakly as she slipped her hand from Kira's and coughed under her breath.

"I saw him change with my own two eyes, and now you've all seen it too."

"That was…" Hawk-Nose licked his lips, turning toward Kira with a calculating grin. "Can you do it again?"

Nine other pale faces turned toward her, and even Luke couldn't seem to avert his gaze.

This is it, Kira thought, *the moment of truth*.

Well, not truth, the moment of amazing fib. The truth was, she had no idea. For all Kira knew, she was turning into a vampire, falling into a pit of darkness so deep that no amount of sunlight could save her. For all she knew, her flames could barely burn a vampire, let alone bring one back from the dead. For all she knew…

"Yes, I can definitely do it again," Kira said, oozing confidence, "but for a price."

Aldrich had to die.

End of story.

"Your war?" Hawk-Nose spoke up again. Kira nodded. Her war.

"And what exactly is it that you want?" A new vampire asked, one who exuded age and wisdom despite his young, brawny appearance.

"Aldrich has threatened not only me, but my friends and family, and he needs to be stopped. We have to kill him."

"And why do you need our help?"

"Because I don't think he's acting alone this time. He

tried it before and almost got destroyed. This time he is coming with reinforcements—"

"Reinforcements who, I might add, we'll need to kill anyway," Pavia interjected. "It's not like the vampire community is really on board with us trying to go backward. We need to show that no one can stop us from becoming human again."

"So we need to find out his plan?" the woman next to Luke asked. He leaned closer to Kira with a slightly green tone to his face.

"Yes, one of you will need to act as a spy to find out what he's up to," Kira affirmed, looking around at the iron faces. "Once we know his plan, we can make our own."

"Any volunteers?" Luke asked, trying to smother his grin when no one jumped for the honor. Kira rolled her eyes and squeezed his knee under the table. That was not helping.

"I will do it," Hawk-Nose said. "But assuming I can infiltrate his group and learn his plan, what assurance do we have that you will follow through? Can you kill him?"

"Yes," Kira said, her voice like ice.

"You've let him go twice before."

"Third time's a charm, right?" No one looked convinced. So Kira swallowed her pride.

He was right, no matter how you looked at it, her track record was bad. The first time, Aldrich had slipped right out of a window at the Red Rose Ball, teasing her with the idea of her mother. But the second time, that was entirely Kira's fault. She let him go to save herself—not to save Tristan, who she hadn't even realized was burning, but to save herself from giving into the evil lurking inside of her.

Was will power enough to keep her sane long enough to kill him this time?

"I'll admit it, all right, Aldrich didn't mysteriously escape in England, I let him go." There was a sharp inhale around the room. "I let him go because I felt Tristan dying." Kira refused to look at Luke, at the confused judgment in his fiery irises. "I felt him burning within my flames and decided it wasn't worth sacrificing his life to end Aldrich's. And even so, I nearly lost him. But with you fighting with me, that won't happen. I can end him—easily."

"Then I will fight with you," Hawk-Nose said.

From the corner of her vision, Kira saw Pavia's lips twitch. Her eyes began to glow a soft royal blue, a satisfied hue.

"I'm in too," Pavia said while reaching for her glass. "Obviously I want a little payback."

The woman beside Luke was next, and then the man next to her joined them. The soft-spoken man across the table from Kira agreed, and within minutes, every vampire in the room had pledged their allegiance—verbally and truthfully.

The funny thing about vampires was you could always call a lie, their eyes said it all. And right then, ten pairs of very bright, very icy blue eyes glowed with life all around the table.

In fact, the only set of eyes looking pissed off rather than excited were the flaming green ones next to Kira—the ones staring her down, reading every lying blush on her face. He knew something was up, that there was something she hadn't told him, something she was hiding from everyone around the table.

But Kira ignored him, because she had her army.

"Why?" Luke asked. Kira kicked him under the table. *What are you doing*, she thought, *be quiet.*

He scooted his chair an inch away from her.

"Why are you all so eager to fight him, to be human?"

"You could never understand," the vampire next to Luke said softly, eyeing him wearily.

"You're right, I don't. I've spent my whole life trying to protect humans from you people, and now instead of killing them, you want to become one?"

"Perhaps I'm tired of all the killing," she said, a sad smile passed over her lips, "but then again, perhaps I'm tired of not caring that a killer is what I've become."

Luke opened his mouth, ready to push forward, his eyes narrowing with suspicion.

"All right then," Pavia said, jumping out of her seat to stop the conversation before it went any further. "Kira, Luke, why don't you crazy conduits get home. I'll walk you out."

Pavia started for the door and Kira grabbed Luke, practically pulling him out of his seat. She didn't say a word until they were outside in the fresh air.

Kira shifted her shoulders back, ready to hold her ground, but before she even opened her mouth, Pavia charged Luke, poking her finger forcefully into his chest.

"All right, Luke. What was that?"

Kira crossed her arms, nodding in agreement and staring Luke down.

"I don't trust vampires," he stubbornly responded, but an apologetic look tugged at his eyes.

"Well we don't trust you either," Pavia said, as though she were talking to an imbecile, "but that doesn't mean we can't do business. Do you want to keep your girlfriend alive or what?"

"Yes," Luke said, "but—"

"Well, if you want her alive then we have to kill Aldrich, and if you want to kill Aldrich you'll need us. In case you didn't realize, the conduits aren't exactly supporting you right now—runaways."

Pavia blew her bangs out of her face, gathering her strength before Luke could get a word in. "And if you're so doubtful, maybe you should just go. We can do this without you."

"Now, wait a minute—"

"No, you wait." Pavia leaned in closer and Luke backed up, his face the definition of shock as she snarled at him. "You want to know why a vampire might want to be human? Take a look at yourself. I know everything in your head. I sense your heart pound every time Kira steps into a room. I feel your blood warm when she meets your stare. I hear the pain tugging at your chest, staggering your breath, when you think about losing her. And did you ever think maybe that's why I want to be human? So I can feel those things for myself without living vicariously through a conduit like you? Vampires can't be in love, and I know Kira doesn't want to hear that but it's true. And what's eternity worth if you're forever alone? Nothing. Absolutely nothing."

Pavia turned to Kira, who flinched under her hard stare. "Kira, I'll see you tomorrow. I owe you some memories before all of the fighting goes down."

And with that, Pavia spun on her heel, whipping Luke in the face with her long, wavy black hair.

Luke, for his part, looked like he had been hit with something far worse—something more like a truck.

"She yelled at me," Luke said, awed.

"Yup, a really good yell too," Kira said, trying not to laugh. A little smile slipped out despite her best efforts.

"I mean, she really yelled at me." He was shell shocked.

"Yeah, well, you deserved it. She kind of stole my thunder actually, I was all prepared to yell at you too."

"But when you yell at me it's cute, when she yells at me…" A shiver traveled down his spine. "It's scary."

"I resent that."

"Hey, wait a second." Luke shifted his gaze to look Kira right in the eye. "I was going to yell at you."

She looked away and started walking down the brick path, back toward the sidewalk outside of the restaurant.

"What was that back there?" he asked, catching up to her quickly.

"What?"

"What? Ha! You know what. Saying you didn't kill Aldrich because of Tristan. I know the truth, you had no idea about Tristan. Why'd you lie? What are you hiding?" Luke took her hand in his, making her stop walking before she opened the door to his car.

Kira didn't meet his stare. She wasn't ready—not to tell him that she might be turning into the one thing he despised most in the world.

And that's when she remembered phase two of tonight's plan. Phase one was complete—she had her army and there was no way Aldrich would escape. But she hadn't even started the next phase, the one to make Luke know that she really loved him too, that she was ready to let Tristan go.

So Kira used the best diversionary tactic she could think of. She grabbed Luke's impatiently waiting face and kissed him.

Success.

Chapter Eight

"Stop!" Kira let go of the steering wheel to slap Luke's hand out of his face.

"Seriously, where are we going?" he said, reaching for his blindfold again.

Kira went in for another slap. "Have you never heard of a surprise before?"

"Maybe I just don't trust you with my car," he said. "It's a man's car."

"Please, I've driven your pickup truck before."

"Okay fine." He sighed. "The not knowing is just killing me. You grab my face, kiss me—not complaining about that at all by the way—and then force a blindfold over my eyes and shove me in the car. I'm not sure if I'm being kidnapped or taken on a date."

"Neither," Kira said, prompting another heavy sigh from Luke, who started tapping his foot against the floor of the car.

"Well if you won't tell me where we're going, will you at least tell me one thing?"

"What?" Kira asked, turning her attention back to the road, which was poorly lit and lined with oak trees. Not exactly ideal for distracted driving.

"Why did you say Tristan was the reason Aldrich escaped?"

Kira sighed. *Not this again.*

"Because I didn't want to tell them the truth."

"Which was?" Luke said, leaving the opening.

"That he got away—that he beat me. We need them on our side." Kira squeezed the steering wheel, and her sweaty palms rubbed harshly against the leather.

She held her breath, waiting for Luke's response.

"I don't buy it."

Kira exhaled angrily. How did he read her so easily? Tristan would have let it go, would have wanted to appease her, but not Luke.

Not wanting to go there, Kira reached out and slipped the knot behind Luke's head free while trying not to crash the car.

"Now I know you're hiding something," he pushed.

"For your information," Kira said, as her palms heated up on the steering wheel and her voice rose an octave, "I was trying to be romantic tonight. So will you just drop it for the time being?"

"For now." He shrugged and turned his gaze out the window. "Are we going to Folly Beach?"

Kira rolled her eyes. So much for the plan.

"Yes, if you must know."

He nodded, biting his bottom lip to keep from grinning.

"What?" Kira asked. He was about to pop, but he shook his head. "What?" she urged.

"It's just..." He started to laugh. "You were supposed to take a right turn about a mile ago."

Kira snarled under her breath, *such a little jerk.* "Do you want to drive too?"

"Are you offering?" He grinned, reaching for the wheel.

"No," Kira snapped, but made the mistake of looking at him. As soon as she spotted his grin, her own mask of anger cracked. "God, you're so annoying." She laughed. "I wanted to be angry at you."

"I know," he chimed, clearly proud with himself. Kira shook her head, trying to quell her smile, but it stayed wide.

Damn, why did he have to be right about that? She squinted, weighing her options, before sighing and making a U-turn in the middle of the empty street.

Luke burst, all intentions of placating her gone. And, after a minute of trying to remain stoic, Kira did too.

"Okay, okay, I'll never play driver again, just bear with me for a few more minutes. We're almost there."

She turned back to the road, blaming Luke's incessant questions for the mistake. A sign up on the left side of the road indicated her next turn, and after a few minutes, Kira was pulling into a sandy parking spot next to the boardwalk. She turned off the engine and stepped out of the car.

Luke followed suit, waiting for her in front of the car since his longer legs carried him faster.

Kira took a deep breath—now or never.

Now, she decided and took Luke's hand, surprised by the sudden swarm of butterflies in her stomach. Beside her, Luke gulped, just loud enough for Kira to hear. He felt it to. The sense that something significant was about to happen, something that might change everything.

Kira led Luke down the boardwalk, each of them silent, listening to the wind ruffle the grassy dunes. The beach was a different place at night. Gone were the crowds, the screaming children, the bright umbrellas, the water wars. It was calm. The waves didn't splash, they rolled, shimmering with starlight. The moon was enough to light a path through soft sand, and Kira followed the trail until her nerves hardened enough to stop her feet from delaying her words any longer.

Luke sensed it before her feet paused. He knew Kira was ready before she herself did, but he was right.

Turning toward the water, Kira bent down until she landed softly in the sand. Luke sunk down next to her, holding onto her hand when she tried to pull away.

A shiver ran down Kira's spine, sending tingles to her limbs.

"You're probably wondering why I wanted to come here?"

Luke shrugged, forcing Kira to continue.

"Well, the thing is…" She paused, thinking. "I guess I just wanted…" She stopped again, rubbing her free hand down the length of her thigh. Why hadn't she planned her speech better?

Kira glanced at Luke, taking comfort in the fire sparkling in his eyes, and suddenly the words fell out.

"You're my best friend, my rock, you know? And that's what this place reminds me of—the day my entire world fell apart, leaving only you to catch me. Tristan was a vampire, my parents were not my parents, I wasn't human, my entire life had been a lie, and everything had changed, but not you. You were there, comforting me, holding me afloat just like always, and I guess that's why I wanted to come here. That day, you became the best friend I've ever had, and I wanted you to know that."

Kira looked at Luke, at the blond hair that still seemed to glow from the sun, at the slightly crooked nose almost completely covered in freckles, at the smile permanently glued to his lips.

"And for what's been almost a year, that's what you've been to me. A best friend. Until I realized something, why wasn't my best friend my boyfriend? When I was in

England, it wasn't Tristan that got me through, it was you, just thinking about you made me feel better. And that's weird, right? And I still do it. Whenever I need to feel better, I sort of peek into your head, and I know I promised I wouldn't read your thoughts anymore, but I do it all the time because it's like taking a little happy pill, and..."

Kira took a deep breath. She was reaching the point of no return.

"And I thought about what you said, at the ball. You said you realized you were in love with me after you thought you'd almost lost me, and I think that's what happened to me too. When I left you in the airport, I thought I'd lost you, that you'd never forgive me, and I didn't know what to do with myself."

God, get to the point, Kira screamed at herself, but she couldn't stop rambling. Why did she feel so exposed? It was Luke, she was never nervous in front of him, but all of a sudden all forms of finesse had escaped her.

"I guess what I'm trying to say is that I don't care that Tristan is human, and I don't care that he doesn't remember me, because I still have you, and I think that's all I ever needed in the first place, and—"

"Kira?"

She swallowed.

"Shut up," Luke said, reaching behind her head to pull her face toward his.

The minute their lips touched, Kira's brain stopped

working. Her mind, already vulnerable, completely let go and Luke's emotions tumbled into her head in a dizzying whirl of lights, a firework show saved just for her.

And Kira wished Luke could feel her thoughts too, the way her excitement bubbled right next to his, sprinkling down her arms, following his every touch. And even though flames weren't sprouting from his hands, they felt on fire as they gripped the back of her neck and traveled down her spine, around to her stomach.

Hungry for more, Kira pushed Luke down, falling with him onto the sand, liking how their bodies molded together. His long lean chest held her weight easily, and his arm wrapped around her back, bringing her closer, slipping under the hem of her shirt to lightly tease her skin.

And the closer they fused, the more Kira felt the sun travel through her body, spreading a warm glow, a sense of peace down her limbs.

Unable to control it, her flames seeped out, circling both of them in her fire. But no longer trapped, the shadows silently followed.

Her blood turned to honey—or was that Luke's blood. His skin felt sweet on her lips, sugary almost.

Kira shifted her lips to his cheek, letting his sigh tremble in her ear. She kissed the line of his jaw, the smooth skin, freshly shaved.

She followed the trail down his throat, the syrupy sweetness teasing her senses, until something began to sing to her, a thrumming pulse, a soft percussion under her tongue...

"Kira?" Luke pushed against her.

She sat up, confused. What was that smell?

"Did you just bite me?"

"What?" she asked, her eyes focusing like lasers on his neck. There was no blood. She let go of her breath, until she saw teeth marks digging into his skin.

"Did you just bite my neck?"

"Um, maybe..." She shifted, leaning away from him. The honey on his skin was still teasing her.

"Why did you just bite me?" he asked, as though speaking to a child.

"I got lost in the moment?" she said, not even convincing herself. Luke's eyebrows furrowed. The excitement in his pupils quickly drained, turning hard and demanding.

"Kira." His voice was a rock, unmoving.

She stood. She had to escape. This was not supposed to happen, not to Luke and her.

Before Kira realized what was happening, she was running. Her feet pounded against solid sand, thumping along with her heartbeat.

Luke yelled after her, but she couldn't stop. It wasn't time. She wasn't prepared to lose Luke right when she had finally found out what he really meant to her.

"Kira!"

Closer this time. He was taller. His legs were longer, faster. Kira veered to the right, searching for a boardwalk in the dunes. Her flight instincts had kicked in, pushing her into overdrive, and all she could think about was getting far away. It didn't matter that he would never stop questioning her, that the next time he saw her he wouldn't let her go. Right now she didn't know what to say or what to tell him.

A hand wrapped around her wrist, jerking her backward. Kira twisted her arm, escaping Luke's hold, but an arm wrapped around her waist, lifting her off the ground. She kicked wildly, doing anything she could.

Luke cursed and dropped her, but almost before her feet hit the ground, he spun her around and hugged her close to his chest.

Kira pounded his muscles with her fists, writhing her body to loosen his hold. Nothing. His arms were iron, trapping her.

"Let me go," she said, still trying to punch her way free.

"Kira, what is going on?"

"I can't." She continued pushing against him, exhausting herself.

"Kira," he soothed, the steel gone from his voice.

"No, Luke," her voice cracked, mirroring the dam breaking inside of her. He was opening the floodgate, but it would be so good to finally talk to someone. But would he ever look at her the same?

Kira's body slumped. All of her energy drained. Luke loosened his hold slightly, just enough to meet her eyes.

"Kira, please talk to me." Concern filled his eyes, dampening the yellow flames around his irises and brightening the warm pine green hues.

"I want to."

"Then do it."

Kira shook her head. Frustration gathered on his face.

"Why not?"

"I can't lose you again," she whispered, clutching at his shirt, trying to make him understand. Her eyes were wide, unblinking, feral.

"You'll never lose me," he said, running his hands up and down her arms to quell the goose bumps gathering there. "I love you, I promise nothing will change that."

"You promise?"

"I promise."

His words were steadfast, but Kira couldn't squish the knot of doubt in the back of her mind. Their bond was open, golden rays of love were pouring in through his mind, but still, Kira knew this would change everything. She was turning. She couldn't deny it or ignore it anymore.

Of all the people in the world, Luke was the only one she could talk to about this but also the last one she wanted to tell. He was her best friend—no he was more than that, so much more. And that was why her mouth hung open, waiting for the words to tumble out, because she didn't want any secrets between them. She had been down that road before and had almost lost him.

So standing there under the stars, wrapped in the warmth of his arms and the sunlight flowing through his veins, she thought for a second that maybe it would all turn out okay…just maybe.

Kira looked up into his steady gaze and took a deep breath. She trusted him more than anyone else in the world. He wouldn't let her down—he never had before.

"I think I'm turning into a vampire…an original vampire."

Luke fell.

His knees collapsed bending outward so he landed Indian style on the ground. Kira dropped onto his lap, probably crushing his legs, but he didn't make a sound. His face was frozen—his lips formed a small surprised circle and his eyebrows bent inward, wrinkling his forehead.

Unsure of what to do, Kira kept talking, not able to stop because every word felt like a weight lifting off of her shoulders. She wasn't alone anymore.

"The Punishers were right. I'm dangerous. I'm falling, just like they said, and it gets worse every day it seems. And it surprises me every time, creeping up on me when I least expect it. And I don't know how to stop it or what to do. When I use my power, I feel the darkness inside of me, trying to escape. And I bit…I bit a vampire. And almost my own mother. And I would have just bitten you if you hadn't stopped me." Kira clutched her head, falling deeper into Luke's chest. "Oh god, what's happening to me? I don't trust myself, and worse, I don't trust my power, my fire, my soul…"

Kira stopped. An ache grew in her head, pressing out from her temples and down her neck. No matter how hard she clutched her hair, the pain wouldn't go away. And she could still smell the sweetness of Luke's blood, could taste it on her tongue.

"How is this possible?" he asked, his voice like sandpaper.

"I don't know."

"I thought…I thought your fire was too strong, that we only had to worry about you losing control, burning too hot…I never imagined…I didn't—when did it start?"

"When Aldrich gave me his blood, something changed inside of me, something dark clung to my heart, and I can't dislodge it." Kira paused, thinking back further, back before she met Aldrich and sighed. "But if I'm being honest with myself, it started a while ago, when my eyes turned blue…when I killed Diana with no remorse and no regret, just satisfaction—the darkness started then, I just didn't feel it."

"And you feel it now?" Luke asked. His blond head lifted. His eyes squinted.

Kira nodded.

"Right now?"

"Always," Kira said softly. Even if it was under control, Kira sensed the sticky black tar hiding in her heart, waiting there for the next opportune moment. "It's one of the reasons I had to leave Sonnyville, there were too many conduits."

"What do you mean?"

She swallowed. Was this the point of no return or had they already passed it?

"Conduit blood." Kira paused when Luke's hand squeezed her arm, almost painfully. "It's the most unbelievable…the most taunting…the sweetest—when I lose control, it's all I can think about."

"And that's why you bit me?"

Kira nodded.

"Is it why you…" Luke took a deep, unsteady breath and closed his eyelids for a moment, thinking. "Is it why you kissed me?"

Kira's eyes widened in shock. "Luke, of course not." She cupped his cheeks with her hands. "I swear, I wanted that, me, Kira."

"Really?"

"Really."

Kira kept hold of his face, urging Luke to believe her. All she had wanted to do tonight was let Luke know that she wanted to be with him, that Tristan wasn't in the picture anymore, but instead she only made him doubt her further. What could she do to make him believe her?

"Luke, I lo—"

He put his pointer finger to her lips, quieting her.

"Not yet, not like this," he said, pain etched in the roughness of his voice. "I've been waiting a long time to hear you say that, and I don't want anything to taint it."

She nodded slowly, fighting her uncertainty.

"Why didn't you tell me sooner?"

Kira laughed under her breath. The situation was anything but funny, but could he hear himself?

He raised his eyebrow, waiting.

"Luke, why do you think? You're freaking out."

"I am not, I'm…digesting."

"Also known as freaking."

"Well, I'm sorry," he said sarcastically, "this is a lot of information for a guy to get all at once. First you kiss me, then you kidnap me, then you kiss me again, then you try to kill me. The signals are getting a little crossed."

"I didn't try to kill you." Kira rolled her eyes. "It was a little nip, some people would find it sexy."

"Some people don't hunt vampires for a living."

"Luke—"

He lifted her around the waist and set her next to him on the sand before standing up. "I need to think," he said and started walking around her in circles. Kira fell back on the ground, not caring that the sand would be stuck in her hair. Looking up at the stars, she began to count the number of times Luke walked around and into her line of vision.

One.

Two.

Three.

She yawned. This was better than counting sheep.

Four.

Five.

Kira waited for number six but it didn't come. She couldn't hear footsteps either. Lifting her body up, Kira scanned the horizon, finding Luke silhouetted against the crashing waves, closer to the surf.

"No," he said suddenly spinning around.

"No, what?" Kira asked, cocking her head to the side as he speedily approached.

"No," he said again, shaking his head. His hands were balled into fists as he passed her and made for the boardwalk ten feet behind Kira.

She quickly stood and chased after him.

"Where are you going?"

"I refuse to let this happen," he said firmly, shouting over his shoulder rather than pausing to turn around.

"You can't stop it," Kira said sadly.

"I can," he urged, "because there is no way in hell that I am finally going to get you, just to watch you turn into a vampire and lose you—there is just no way that is happening. I won't allow it."

"Luke." Kira sighed.

Her insides felt all mushy after his sweet words—

totally macho and unrealistic words, but sweet all the same.

"No, Kira, there has got to be something we can do."

"Luke, there's nothing. I checked the papers my grandfather gave me, the ripped out pages, they didn't say anything about this. I can feel this thing growing inside of me all the time. It won't stop."

He stopped walking, spinning around so fast that Kira ran right into his chest.

"Who are you right now?" He was incredulous.

"Huh?"

"Where is Kira? Where's my best friend? She would never just give up and let this happen without a fight."

"I," Kira started but stopped. He was right. What was she doing?

"Your parents!" His entire face lit up with the idea. Luke clutched her shoulders, shaking her a little. "Your parents, they have to know something."

"My dad doesn't even know I'm a conduit," Kira said slowly, trying to understand.

"No." Luke shook his head, widening his eyes with exasperation. "Your birth parents. Your dad was a Punisher. The first time you used your powers, he must have suspected this might happen, he must have known the legends."

"My birth parents…" Kira said slowly, her brain going haywire with new ideas suddenly taking life. Maybe there was a cure, some sort of solution. But Luke wasn't waiting for her to catch up.

"The original conduits, the angels the Punishers speak of all the time, they changed themselves, they figured it out. There's got to be a way." Luke spun again, walking briskly toward the car.

Kira raced to catch up, running toward the car, but a thought stopped her in her tracks.

"Pavia," Kira said. Why hadn't she thought of it before?

"What?" Luke asked. He was next to his pickup truck, holding the passenger side door open for her.

"Pavia has all of my mother's memories," Kira said, slowly raising her gaze to meet Luke's excited and flaming eyes. "If my parents knew anything—"

"Pavia will know," he said, cutting her off. "Give me the keys."

Kira tossed them toward him. He caught them in one graceful move before hopping into the driver's seat.

"Call her," he said, turning on the ignition.

The engine rumbled to life beneath her—somehow it gave her hope.

"Tell her we need to talk immediately."

Chapter Nine

Kira raced through the front door of Luke's house, not even pausing to say hello to a shocked Tristan before yelling out, "Pavia?"

No answer. Shoot.

Luke strolled through a few seconds later, much calmer.

"Is everything all right?" Tristan asked, sitting up straighter on the couch. A history textbook was open on his lap.

"Yeah," Kira said, taking off her shoes and falling into the open spot next to him, "we just have a few questions to ask Pavia."

"Is there anything I can do?"

"Nope." Kira looked at him, forcing out a strained smile. "But thanks for asking."

"Of course," he said, taking her hand. The warmth

felt strange to Kira, so she stood up, slipping out of his grasp.

"Anyone want something while we wait? I'm making some coffee."

"Make that two," Luke said, looking away from the window he was staring at.

"Tristan?"

"If you have any tea…"

"Sure thing," Kira said and left the room. She bit her lip while searching Luke's cabinets. Her excitement was getting hard to contain. Why hadn't she thought of it before? Her parents. Of course they had to know something. But no, Kira chided and started the coffee pot, it was too early to get her hopes up.

She put her hands palm down on the counter, stilling them against the cold stone, willing the tremble in her fingers to stop.

Her foot started tapping instead.

"So, what's the big emergency?"

"Pavia!" Kira jumped, clutching at her heart. The vampire was standing in Luke's back door, waiting to be let inside. Hastily, Kira pulled at the handle. "Thank god you're here."

"That's not something I hear very often." Pavia grinned, flipping a stray lock back over her forehead.

The coffee pot dinged, making Kira jump again.

"Did I hear…" Luke popped his head around the

corner, smiling when he saw Pavia there. "Come on into the living room," he urged, acting suddenly hospitable.

Kira gave him a cup of coffee and followed the two of them into the other room, stopping to give Tristan his tea before taking up the same spot on the couch. Pavia and Luke sat opposite them on two chairs.

"So what happened in the past two hours that's got you both so wired?" Pavia's eyes went to Luke's twiddling thumbs and Kira's ticking foot.

"It's probably easier to show you," Kira said and reached her arm out. "Just take a look at my most recent memory."

Pavia raised her eyebrows, surprised, but brushed Kira's fingers with her own.

Instead of a rushing vortex, there was a numbness that settled over Kira's body, a feeling like she wasn't in control of her own mind anymore. Something crawled over her skin, fuzzing up her thoughts and sending a shiver down her spine.

Pavia pulled back.

"Are you serious?"

"What's going on?" Tristan asked meekly.

"Kira here, the same Kira who promised to turn me and about a dozen other scary vampires into humans, is turning into a freaking original vampire!"

Oh right, Kira swallowed, she had momentarily forgotten about that promise.

"It's okay, I'll be able to turn you," she said, trying to calm Pavia down.

"Oh really? You could barely even make out with Blondie over here before going psycho conduit."

"She'll be able to do it," Luke pressed, "but we need your help."

"Well, what else is new?"

"If you want to be human, I'll make it happen, I promise," Kira said, leaning in toward the currently freaking out vampire.

"How?"

"We think there might be a cure," Luke said.

"You think?"

"This is where we need your help." Kira sighed. "I need to cash in on those memories." A little twinge of pain zapped her chest. She had been hoping for more memories of her parents, but not like this. She had wanted to enjoy them, to get to know her family, not rush through with an ulterior motive.

"What do you need to see?"

"My father was a Punisher. We think maybe he always knew this might happen, that maybe he knew something." Kira paused, licking her suddenly dry lips. "Can you see if my mom ever talked to him about it?"

"That's not a very strong lead," Pavia said, doubtful.

"Please." Luke lifted his head, looking at the vampire—a hint of desperation edged into his words, a slightly lost look leaked into his fiery eyes. "Please, it's all we have."

Pavia met his look, hesitating, before releasing a huge exhale and shaking her head. "Jeez, when did I become such a softie? I need my vampire mojo back."

"So you'll help?" Kira asked.

She blew her ebony bangs from her forehead. "Yes, I'll help. But you better be able to turn me human when all of this is over, because this whole compassionate thing doesn't work so well in my world."

"Done," Kira said, pursing her lips to keep from grinning like a little girl. She flicked her eyes to Luke, who was already staring at her, beaming like the sun itself. Warmth flowed through the bond, sinking into her limbs, filling her with hope. It wasn't over, not yet.

"You two are sickening," Pavia said while standing up. "Give me a minute to see if I can find anything."

Kira nodded absently, not breaking contact with Luke. Why hadn't she told him earlier? Of course he would know what to do. He had this way of solving all of her problems.

"Kira?" a soft voice asked.

Tristan, Kira thought, *crap*. She had totally forgotten he was there. How horrible was she?

"I'm sorry." She looked at him, reading the confused wrinkles in his face, the slight squint to his warm, questioning brown eyes. "God, we should have explained this to you before we told Pavia anything. It's just…"

What could she say? It's just that he didn't understand anymore? It's just that he didn't belong in this world anymore? It's just that she didn't know how to talk to him anymore?

"I don't want you to worry about me." Kira settled on that. "You have enough on your plate already."

"Worrying about you feels sort of natural," he said, the hint of a smile on his lips. Kira rolled her eyes. That was so…Tristan. But it was nice at the same time, nostalgic almost.

"You don't have to." She squeezed the hand next to hers on the couch. "I have this odd feeling that maybe everything will work out." She flicked her eyes to Luke quickly. "For all three of us."

Kira glanced at Pavia, still pacing behind the couch. Maybe it would work out for all four of them, if Kira could keep it together long enough.

Pavia stopped walking.

"I might have found something—"

"What?" Kira interrupted, her eagerness getting the best of her.

Pavia gave her a pointed look—it seemed to say please shut up. "Am I showing both of you or just Kira?"

"Me."

"Both of us."

Luke and Kira spoke at the same time.

Pavia glanced at her, smirking. *Whoops*, Kira thought and coughed. "Uh, both of us."

"Let's do this, then."

Kira nodded and so did Luke. Tristan picked his book up again, and though it hurt Kira not to include him, this wasn't his life anymore. Or she hoped it soon wouldn't be.

Pavia scooted her chair over and put her hands out. Locking eyes, Kira and Luke reached out at the same time, completing the bond.

And like the last time Kira had connected with her mother's memories, instead of falling, it was as though she were floating, drifting calmly down like a feather in a spring breeze. It was a gentle process. The thoughts welcomed her, sensed that she was family, that maybe she was meant to be there. Rainbows danced before her, blurring Luke's living room and kaleidoscoping her vision. Cool and warm colors mixed together with no rhyme or reason, twisting and turning through a slowly moving prism, until slowly the blue drifted to the peripheral, disappearing entirely. The greens faded next, leaking slowly from Kira's vision. The reds and oranges softened to a dark umber, and the purples shifted to an ebony black. The yellow stayed bright and vibrant, flickering before her almost like a…and suddenly Kira was there, visiting her mother in the only way she ever would…

Fire, it always came down to fire. The fire sparking in the hearth of their small concealed cabin, the flames just minutes ago dancing on her palm, or the ones she knew were hiding inside of the little baby girl asleep on her chest. Everything in her world always seemed to come down to fire.

Three days—her world had changed exponentially in such a short amount of time. But she was home, because their little cabin in the woods finally felt like a home to her now that her newly born daughter was there, resting on her chest, making this whole life seem real for the first time.

"Lana?"

"Shh," she called softly to her husband, Andrew, "I think she might be asleep." Her daughter's tiny little eyes were closed. Her almost impossibly small hand had loosened its hold and was now resting softly on her mother's chest, right next to her heart.

Three days ago, this baby was inside of her. But now she was here, breathing, smiling, squirming. It was all real—all of those dreams.

Andrew footsteps thudded against the wooden floors of their small home. Even in socks, her husband wasn't great at being quiet. But the thought triggered a different memory, of the first time they met, causing a little grin to crease her lips.

He sat down next to her on the couch, dipping the cushion with his added weight. Their baby stirred, shifting slightly in her mother's arms before stilling once more.

Deep grooves cut into Andrew's forehead, making him look older than the young man she had married just a few months before. Then again, life had moved along very quickly for the two of them, faster than was really fair, but she wouldn't change a thing.

She shifted slightly, making sure not to distress the baby, and leaned into his solid chest.

"No change?" he whispered. She shook her head. No change—their baby still didn't show signs of having powers, no fire spilled from her adorable little fingers. But she sensed that it was only a matter of time, that their daughter was stronger than either of them realized.

"Good." He sighed. A little prick of pain pinched her chest to hear him say it. "Everything will be easier this way, we won't have to hide."

No, *she thought*, we won't have to hide from our people, but if our daughter doesn't have powers, won't we have to hide from her? *She would rather run from the conduits for the rest of her life than hide their heritage from the little girl sleeping in her arms. Maybe it was a mother's dream, but she didn't want secrets to stain their family.*

But wait.

What was that?

She looked down. Almost as if summoned by her thoughts, a soft glow surrounded her little girl's palm.

"Andrew?" she whispered, not looking away. Was she seeing things? But no, she felt it, felt the heat from the palm on her chest, small as it was, the flames were strong as they sank into her heart. "Andrew," she said more urgently, waking him from whatever thoughts tugged at his mind.

"What?"

"Look."

She shifted the baby ever so slightly, but enough that a sliver of fire broke free, rising up, crackling in the still air rather than sinking into her skin. The baby shifted back, sealing the gap again, but not before she heard a gasp.

Excited, she looked up, but her heart immediately sank.

Her husband's eyes were full of dread, widening with a fear she didn't understand. His mouth opened, but no words came out. He just stared at the baby in her arms, until a tremble stirred his hands.

"Andrew?" She didn't understand. Why wasn't he happy? "What is it?"

"Nothing." He shook his head, shaking whatever had been gathering in his mind. "Nothing."

She didn't believe him. He was hiding something from her.

"What is it?"

"Nothing, just a stupid, nothing. Let me hold her," he said and reached his hands out, easily holding their daughter as they made the transfer. As soon as their little girl was in his arms, his body slackened. The tension in his limbs fell away, and a wide grin spread across his cheeks.

"She's strong," he said, moving so the fire warmed his heart as well.

"I knew she would be."

"Me too," he said, but somehow the words were tainted.

Stop, she told herself. Nothing would ruin this moment, this moment when everything she had dreamed of for the past few months had become real. They were a family—a real, united, unbreakable family.

Kira blinked and she was back. A chill shivered up her limbs from the lack of fire. The room was cold, or maybe it was just the absence digging at her heart. Once again, they were gone, pulled away from her, dead—it was like losing her parents all over again. Her mother's mind was a warm blanket, making her feel safe and loved, but it had been ripped away.

Another chill crept down her spine.

She wanted to feel the warmth again.

Kira looked up, meeting Pavia's concerned eyes, but looked away. She knew what those eyes were saying, what memory they were referencing. The last time Kira had shared her mother's thoughts, she had begged Pavia to see them again, even offered her own blood in exchange for another memory. But England was another time, that castle had made her feel so alone. Here, now, the warm palm on her knee was keeping her grounded. Or really, the man it was connected to.

Kira followed the line, running right into Luke's flaming irises, and they were enough to spark her back to life.

"My father knew something."

"I think so too," Luke said, squeezing her leg gently.

"Pavia, is there anything else?"

The vampire shook her head. "I was looking quickly, but that was the most obvious thing I saw. He was definitely afraid of something, thinking of something he didn't want your mom to know about, but I don't know what that is. There were a few more memories of him leaving the cabin, going to meet with the conduits, and coming back frustrated. But nothing specific. I'm sorry."

"But Kira," Luke urged, seeing her shoulders slump, "it's a start."

But the start of what? If he had truly found some answers, would he have told her mother? Would he have said something?

Kira stood and started pacing. Something about moving her legs made the wheels in her drained mind spin.

If the answers weren't in Pavia's mind, where would they be? *Think, Kira, think.* Would her adoptive mother know something? Would her brother have confided in his sister? But no, she would have mentioned something—"hey my daughter might at some point turn into a deadly vampire" wasn't exactly the kind of conversation anyone would forget.

But if he was concerned and he did think that might happen, wouldn't he have looked for answers? Kira was stubborn, and considering her parents had gotten married, run away from home, and had a practically illegal child, she had a pretty strong feeling they were as well. So if he thought this might happen, he would have looked for answers. Kira knew he would have.

"Research," she said, stopping in her tracks to clutch the back of the couch.

"Of course," Luke said, looking up from behind his clenched fingers.

"Huh?" Pavia said, eyebrow raised in question.

"It's so obvious! He was doing research. He never met with the conduits. My mother, or I mean my aunt, she told me ages ago that once they ran away, my parents had stopped talking to everyone, even her. So if he was leaving, he wasn't going to talk to the council, he was doing research."

"And if he was researching…" Luke stood too, his excitement mounting with Kira's. "He has to have notes somewhere. Probably hidden from your mom, since he clearly wanted to keep her out of it."

"But where?" Kira asked.

"Kira." Luke looked at her, widening his eyes as the idea in his mind grew. "The cabin."

"The cabin!" she gasped.

"The cabin?" Pavia interjected. "The one from your mom's memories? It's been eighteen years since they died, that place is long gone."

"You don't know that," Kira said, grinning so much her cheeks hurt. "It was in a hidden location. Even if looters saw it or someone else lives there now, he could have hidden papers under the floorboards or in a trapped enclosure or something. We have to—"

"I know," Luke said.

"But wh—"

"Tomorrow."

"With—"

"We need your mom."

Kira pulled the phone from her pocket, dialed her mother's phone number, and started pacing again. Her arms tingled with excitement—a new energy, a hopeful energy, was buzzing all around her insides.

"Hello?"

"Mom!" Kira shouted, and then winced. "Sorry, sorry."

"It's okay! Are you all right? Things have been crazy around here. The councils, the Punishers, I have so much to tell you. They—"

"Mom, Mom, hold on, let me go first." Her mother stayed silent, so Kira plowed on. "The cabin, the one where my birth parents lived, do you know how to find it? Do you think it's still there?"

"Maybe, but it's been a while, honey, I doubt it's even there anymore. Andrew, he wasn't exactly a master builder, and I only went once. I always meant to go back, to get their things, but there was never any time."

"We're going," Kira said, "and before you start arguing, it's really, really important. And if I tell you why, you're just going to freak, so it would be much easier if you just told us where to go and met us at the airport."

"That's not exactly how the whole parent child thing works," her mother drawled. "Tell me what's going on, and

I mean right now, or Kira, you will finally get all of the punishments you've been earning these last few months. And I mean it. There'll be no money, no cars, no cooking school, no—"

"Mom, I'm turning into a vampire."

There was a long pause. If not for the steady breathing, Kira would have thought her mother had hung up. She felt a little guilty for just throwing it all out there, but really, the motherly rant had been fast approaching— dire measures needed to be taken.

"Kira, you," she started but then stopped.

After a minute, Kira asked, "Mom?"

"You just, you can't just say something like that and expect me to be okay."

Kira rolled her eyes. "I don't expect you to be okay, in fact I expect you to be so concerned that you'll jump on a plane and meet me wherever we need to go." She smiled sweetly out of habit, almost as though her mother could see her.

A heavy sigh came through the line.

"You're as infuriating as my brother," she said, and then, "Meet me at the Greenbrier Valley Airport in West Virginia, do you have that? Greenbrier Valley?"

"Got it, I'll let you know as soon as Luke and I have flights."

"Kira?"

"Yeah?"

"I love you, but really, when all of this is done, you're grounded."

"Okay, Mom." Kira rolled her eyes. Her adoptive parents had never been great at punishing her. Maybe because until this year she had never really needed to be punished, having been in boarding school.

"Don't you roll your eyes at me." *What the?* Kira thought, *how does she know?* "I'm your mother, I know you. And I mean it. When all of this is over, vampires are going to be the least of your worries."

"Okay, Mom," she repeated in a much graver tone. "I really am sorry. I love you."

"I love you too. Call me as soon as you can."

"Deal."

Kira hung up the phone, meeting Luke's eyes. They had a lot to do if they were going to be in West Virginia before the sun rose.

Chapter Ten

Kira looked around the airport. Her mom should be here by now. Had something happened? Did Aldrich's cronies come back? Was she trapped somewhere? Alone and helpless?

"Kira."

She jumped... not helpless, just angry...

"Mom! I'm so happy you're here."

"Yeah, yeah." She gave her daughter a quick hug. "I know what your punishment is going to be." Kira rolled her eyes. Really? The first words out of her mouth?

Next to her, Luke snickered. Jerk. She should have left him back in Charleston with Pavia and Tristan.

"Was it that you got to fly air-conduit on the private jet while Luke and I were stuck in smaller than half-of-my-butt-cheek seats next to the bathroom? Did I mention the flush was broken?"

"It was traumatizing, Mrs. D," Luke said in a

sorrowful voice.

"No, that's not it." She grinned. "But it does make me feel a little better."

"Mom." Kira rolled her eyes and started walking ahead of them toward the rental car stand. She was evil.

"First, you're staying home for a while, I mean until you go to the college or culinary school of your choice." Kira started to protest but was waved off. "There are plenty of wonderful restaurants to work at in Charleston."

Kira sighed but nodded. Charleston was a great city and she wanted to spend more time with her family anyway. "Second?" Better to get it over with.

"Second, no trips, not even with Luke or the conduits, unless I'm there too."

"But—"

"No buts, I'm serious."

"Okay," Kira said through gritted teeth. *Please let third be last.*

"Finally, you're getting a curfew. After finding out Tristan was a vampire, and right under my nose all this time, I just can't trust you yet. So home by eleven every night, unless it's a special occasion and you ask me for permission a week in advance—with a convincing argument."

Part of Kira wanted to stomp her foot in annoyance, but a bigger part of her understood and kept the temper tantrum inside. To a lot of people, this would be considered almost lenient for lying about traveling to a foreign country, dating a member of the undead, and, well, a few more things that Kira couldn't quite keep track of.

She put out her hand.

"Deal. When all of this is over and Aldrich is dead, I'll come home and be your own personal hermit."

Her mom took her hand and shook it. But before letting go, she tugged her daughter in for a hug. "I missed you, and I love you, don't ever forget that."

Kira smiled into her mom's shoulder. "I love you too."

With a sniffle, her mother let her go and went to stand in line for a rental car.

A few seconds later, Luke's warm breath tickled her neck, sending a delicious shiver down her spine.

"So," he whispered, "do we tell your parents about us, or for the next year am I still the best friend who's allowed in your bedroom with the door closed?"

Kira turned, grinning. "Well, I did just agree to stop lying to my parents…"

Luke pouted, letting his puppy-dog eyes droop downward in a very convincing argument. Kira put a hand on his chest, using the balance to rise on her toes, bringing her lips to his ear.

"I'm game if you are."

She dropped down quickly, taking a step back before her mother saw anything. And it was just in time, because as Kira turned, her mother was finishing up with the agent.

Waving, Kira and Luke made their way over and followed her mother out the door. As they settled inside the off-road SUV, the one her mom had specially ordered, the nerves began—a little swarm of bees buzzing in her stomach. She was going home, to her first home, to the home she only remembered in stolen thoughts and barely there dreams.

"Okay, talk," her mom said as she revved the engine. Kira didn't need an explanation and with a sigh, she started telling the story—the whole story, starting all the way back with the eclipse, the fight with Diana, the cause of her coma, the Red Rose Ball, the trip to England, the moment she started to feel the change within herself, the darkness.

The only part Kira kept out, the one part she couldn't even speak about, was the fight right outside of Sonnyville just days earlier. There was no way she could tell her mother that she had almost bitten her, that she had tried to eat her. The mere thought made her insides cramp, made bile gather on her tongue, made...

Kira stopped thinking about it, pushed the memory away, and looked at her mother.

With each passing minute, the older woman's face darkened a little more—with worry or anger, Kira wasn't sure. At times, it looked like she wanted to say something, would open her mouth just to close it again or widen her eyes just to squint once more.

In the end, all her mother did was reach out her hand

and intertwine their fingers, but it was perfect. It was exactly what Kira needed. Not another lecture or another punishment or another fight, just the support and understanding that only a mother could provide.

And they stayed like that for Kira didn't know how long, because her attention had shifted out the window, away from Luke and her adoptive mother and Tristan and conduits and vampires and Aldrich. Her attention was long gone, running ahead of the car, following her heart home to the parents she had never gotten the chance to know.

Kira didn't notice as the city began to fade. She didn't see the dense forest that took its place. She no longer felt her mother's fingers or the subtle peace flowing in from Luke's mind. All she felt was an overwhelming sense of déjà vu, and maybe it was just her mind playing tricks, but somehow she sensed that she had been to this place before.

A tune started singing inside her head, a lullaby, soothing, a woman's voice. The image before her flickered, phantom flames danced in its place. The comforting smell of burnt wood filled her nostrils. And maybe even the dull thud of heavy boots walking through the front door…

"Kira, honey?" A warm palm landed on her shoulder. Her mother.

"Huh?" Kira blinked. The image was gone, the memory, if she could call it that. Or was is just another thing she borrowed from her birth mother? Another thought she had peeked at in Pavia's mind?

"Kira, we need to walk the rest of the way."

She nodded and drowsily slipped out of the car, not yet with it. They had parked on the shoulder, tucked against the trees in a narrow opening along the road.

"It's been a long time since I was here, Kira, I'm not sure I'll even be able to find the place." She looked worried and shifted her head around the tree line.

"It's okay, Mom," Kira urged, "we just have to try."

Her mom walked ahead, looking for familiar landmarks.

Luke slipped his hand in hers, squeezing once before letting it go, very aware of the parental presence close by.

"Are you okay?" He leaned down to whisper in her ear.

"I think so."

"You seemed pretty quiet back in the car." He waited for her, listening for even a sigh in response.

"Would you think I'm crazy if I said I might remember this place? That it somehow feels familiar?" Kira looked at the ground, drawing a little circle in the grass with her toe.

"Of course not," Luke said and gently guided her chin upward, arching her head toward his. Concern and affection flooded his features. "I'd say that's amazing."

"I think it's pretty awesome, too." Her eyes crinkled in a barely there smile. It was more than amazing—it was almost magical.

"I think it might be this way," her mother called, indicating a space between two large trees. Luke and Kira eased apart, making their way over as her mom disappeared into the trees.

Wherever they were going, it looked pretty deserted. There were no footsteps on the ground. There was no lightly traveled dirt path, no wrappers leftover from a camping trip or signs pointing where to go. There was grass and dirt and shrubs and leaves and sticks—pretty much everything an animals-only forest might contain.

And with the need to concentrate on where she was stepping, Kira pretty much gave up on recognizing anything. Staring at the ground was all she had time for.

"You know," Luke said behind her as they stepped over a particularly large pool of squishy mud, "England was almost a nice break. You were living in a gigantic castle, I was cooped up in a nice flat in the heart of London—not too shabby—but somehow, we're back here, ankle deep in I don't even know what."

"Look at you, turning into a prima donna."

"I'm just saying, when all of this is over and you're on house arrest, don't expect me to sneak through the miniature forest in your backyard anytime soon."

"That is something we can definitely agree on," Kira said, grimacing as her shoe sank an inch into the ground. Thank goodness she was wearing sneakers.

Up ahead, her mom gasped and stopped moving.

Kira stopped too, and then broke off at a sprint, no longer caring about the mud caking her feet.

In seconds, she had caught up to her mom. Barely a foot in front of her, Kira stopped again. Her heart jumped in her chest, no longer able to sustain any movement because her whole body was stuck, frozen in place, halted on the breath caught in her throat.

The cabin.

It was standing.

It was there, right before her very eyes, visible through the sea of tree trunks.

Kira ran again, because it all came crashing down, every minute she had dreamed of her parents, of their lives together, of the memories hidden deep within her own head. All of it landed on her in a tidal wave of momentum pushing her feet forward, until it was too much, and she tripped and fell right before the front doorway.

"Kira, wait!"

But she couldn't.

Jumping to her feet, Kira lunged up the steps, taking two at a time until her fingertips were wrapped around a rusty doorknob.

Taking a deep breath, Kira closed her eyes, keeping them tightly shut in fear that it was all just a dream.

She twisted.

The door swung open, creaking on unused hinges.

She was trembling. What if she opened her eyes and

nothing was there but more disappointment, more confusion? What if…

Enough. Her eyelids slid open.

There was dust everywhere—a thick gray layer covering the wooden floor, the holey rug, the single chair laying on its side. Windows were broken. The roof was caving inward, dented from a fallen tree still leaning on the house. Vines of ivy and little shrubs broke through the wood in various spots, turning the space into an indoor garden.

But Kira didn't see any of that.

Kira saw a living room and a kitchen and the door to a tiny bedroom. She saw her father sitting on a couch, her mother rocking her in a chair, flames glowing in the fireplace.

Walking forward, Kira put her hand on the rocker. The wood was smooth under the dust now staining her fingertips. Kira pulled, bringing the seat back to its feet, and sat. Mud already caked her shoes—the dust clinging to her pants didn't matter.

Pushing lightly against her toes, Kira closed her eyes and let the world shift around her, undulating softly while the wooden floor squeaked in protest. And with one long breath, phantom arms encircled her body, giving her the hug she had dreamed of. They were thin, fragile, but still strong. The arms of a fighter and a mother all in one.

Lips pressed softly against her hairline, lovingly, like a

father might do to wish his daughter goodnight if he thought she was asleep. A large hand landed softly on her shoulder, squeezing gently, comforting her, lending her strength.

Kira pulled on the chain around her neck, feeling blindly for the locket, slipping her finger through her father's wedding ring.

Love will prevail.

She had never forgotten those words. And in this moment, Kira understood why. Even though they were gone, even though this house was one step away from ruin, even though Kira didn't really remember them, she could feel their love. Her every breath was full of it. Her chest was heavy but the air was light, playful, happy, endless.

Footsteps thudded behind her.

Kira's eyes flew open. She jumped out of the rocker, throwing her gaze toward the front door.

It was Luke...only Luke.

Disappointment stabbed at her. Stupid, she chided, of course it was Luke. But the little girl inside of her—the vulnerable, parent-less child—heard other feet, wished for different times.

Her aunt followed behind him, and in this place, it seemed right to call her an aunt and not a mother, even if it wasn't fair. And Kira knew it wasn't.

Kira swallowed deeply, dropping her locket back under her shirt. She tasted salt on her lips and wiped her cheeks clean, erasing the girl and bringing the half-breed conduit back to life. They were here to do a job.

"Kira, you have to be careful," her aunt said softly, frozen in the doorway, seemingly stuck in place, "the house isn't stable."

"We don't have to stay long," Kira said. Her voice was cold, empty. The only way to get through the aching loss that seemed to choke her was to smother it under a blanket of ice. "Let's start searching for anything that might be useful."

Luke frowned at her tone, but nodded and stepped farther into the tiny house.

"It looks like someone might have been here a long time ago, like maybe they looted the place," he said while he surveyed the space. Kira followed his line of vision to the lack of furniture, the lack of any personal items.

"Mom, keep watch. Luke, look around in here." She had to get away from the fireplace, from her mother's memories. "I'll go into the other room."

Without waiting for a response, Kira shuffled through the door and into the next room. A broken bed frame lay crumpled in the middle of the floor. The mattress was long gone. A dresser was pulled apart right next to the entry. Kira hesitated a centimeter from the unstained wooden knobs, before clutching them and pulling the drawer fully out. Empty. She closed it, fighting against the imperfectly cut wood, wondering distantly if her father had built it.

The next drawer was empty too. Kira jammed it shut, ignoring the sound of slamming wood. One drawer left.

She yanked on it, but it only came out halfway. Excited, Kira pulled harder, falling back on the floor when the drawer suddenly sprung free and slipped completely out of the dresser, landing with a smack at her feet.

Empty except for a piece of shredded cloth.

Kira started to curse, but paused and reached for the sliver. It was silk, maybe four inches wide and ten inches long, with small, multicolored flowers printed against a black backdrop. Kira rubbed the smooth cloth between her fingers, pressing it lightly to her cheek, wondering what it might have been—an old blouse? A scarf that got ripped while a robber hastily tried to pull it free of the drawer?

Kira tucked the scrap in her pocket, standing slowly back to her feet. She still had a job to do, but the only other piece of furniture in the room was a small nightstand, both levels of which were completely bare.

She and Luke had been naïve to think the cabin would have gone untouched all of these years. It was idiotic really, to think that the cabin would stay a secret forever. Maybe hungry campers had happened upon the spot, used the food, realized the place was abandoned, and taken the clothes. Maybe they reported it to some official who came and cleared the space out, selling everything in a big yard sale, making money for the local government. What if strangers had pored over their items? Over her parents priceless items? Kira would have given her life savings for just one photo, one book that held their fingerprints, one necklace that told their story...

Someone out there could be wearing her mother's shoes, or her father's coat—could be sitting on their couch or eating with their silverware.

The injustice hit Kira like a wave, surging through her entire body, swelling to a breaking point. She needed the release, she needed to explode, but even in this sacred place, the taint of her flames hit her.

The anger bubbled up, but Kira was afraid to let it out the way her heart told her to. Her palms burned, but the shadows were there too, lurking, and no one would be around to stop her this time. Even now, Kira sensed Luke in the other room, and more faintly her mother—the scent of their blood getting stronger as her powers gathered inside of her.

So she did the only thing she could think of...she kicked the bed really, really hard, yelling as the pain hit her toe, sending a flash up her spine. But in an odd way it felt good, it felt better than anger, so Kira kicked again, just to feel connected to the real world. And she kicked again...and again...crying and screaming now...and again, until the post broke in half and the entire frame crashed to the floor with a loud thud.

"Kira," Luke said, hesitant and unsure. He touched her arm, barely brushed her skin with his fingers, but Kira spun into the hug he was offering, crushing her face into his warm chest, letting his body catch the sobs, and using his shirt to muffle the sounds she didn't really understand were coming from her body.

He ran his fingers through her hair, somehow managing to navigate her curls so the strokes were smooth, calm, reassuring. He lightly kneaded her back, making the tension in her body ease away. And he sent his light into her body, both physically and through their connection, encasing her in a shell of warmth, in a circle of fire that felt almost like hers, except for its purity.

After a few minutes, Kira stepped away from him, sniffling, afraid to meet his eyes. But Luke knew her well enough to let her retreat and regain her composure.

"Did you?"

Luke shook his head.

"Me neither."

Kira sighed. Her toe ached. They had nothing.

"You did a pretty thorough job of killing the evil bed frame though."

A smile tugged at Kira's lip.

"Demon Witch. Flaming Tomato. Feared by bed posts everywhere."

The grin pulled wider. Luke poked her, prodding another wide stretch.

Kira looked at him, meeting his smiling, twinkling eyes. "Thanks." And then she looked away, toward the post, now broken in half on the ground. "I didn't know I was that strong."

"Eh, old wood." Luke shrugged.

"But it's a little strange, right?" Kira said, an idea sparking. She stepped closer, looking at the bottom of the broken post.

A circle.

There was a circle cut into the wood.

"Luke!" She gasped, reaching for the piece of broken wood. Her fingers fit perfectly into the opening, and there, Kira felt something smooth.

Could it possibly be?

Yes, it was paper.

Kira tried to grip it, sliding the pages against the rough wood. She slammed the post against her palm, until the paper tapped her skin. A bundle fell into her hand.

Kira unrolled it. Handwriting. Scrawls of pen spanned the pages. She flipped to the next and there were more of them.

"We found it," Kira said in disbelief. Was it too much to hope? "We found it!" she said again, more excited.

Luke gripped her upper arms, his face a sea of changing expressions, finally settling on adoration. "You found it, Kira! You—"

Unable to speak anymore, Luke pulled her toward him, landing his lips on hers because there was nothing else he could do. Speech had escaped him.

Kira started laughing against his lips, a joyous sound, the sound of possibility, of her future somehow open again. Almost like he expected it, Luke simultaneously joined her—a deep tenor to her soprano, the perfect song.

They pressed their foreheads together, sighing in unison to catch their breaths, pausing for a moment to look at eternity in each other's eyes—

A scream pierced through the cabin. A scream Kira had heard before.

Her mother, her adoptive mother. The sound came from outside, traveling through a broken window and into her ears. She dropped the papers.

Fire tickled her palms.

Kira raced past Luke, out the front door, as he scrambled to pick up the discarded research and catch up.

Somehow, vampires had managed to find them.

And knowing there would somehow be a cure, Kira didn't really feel the need to slow the flames bursting from her palms.

Chapter Eleven

Dead.

They were all dead the second that Kira stepped out of that door. It was just that none of them knew it yet.

The flames traveling down her arms were all Punisher, were all meant to kill, and Kira just didn't care anymore. She felt the smoke, the black fog drifting in wispy tendrils around her fire. The darkness was there, lurking. The vampire dormant inside of her was looking for a way to take over. But there was a cure. And there were vampires outside who needed to die, not just be forced away by Luke's Protector powers.

When she stepped through the door, Kira barely registered the vampire clutching her mother's head, bending it to the side to reveal a pearly, untouched throat. She didn't count the number of eyes watching, there were too many to take in. All she did was let it out—all of her power—

something she hadn't allowed herself to do in what seemed like forever.

Before the vampires knew Kira was there, they were burning in her powers, melting into ash, until all that was left had disappeared into the wind. But there were more. Kira could feel them, could almost see their glowing eyes in the shadows.

Luke rushed out behind her, surveying the damage she had already dealt.

"Kira—"

"Get my mom and keep her safe."

He hesitated for a second before nodding and jumping down the steps. He helped her mother stand and brought her closer to the house, until his back touched the wood.

Kira's eyes didn't stop scanning the trees. She trusted Luke, trusted him to keep her mother alive. He wouldn't let her down, so Kira would do her part to keep them all alive.

To her left, a vampire jumped out. Kira's hand flew on its own, casting flames so fast that the vampire evaporated before her feet even touched the ground.

On her right, another one. Kira shot out again, controlling her fire the best she could. Back to her left she saw movement.

"Above you!" She heard Luke's voice shouting into her head before the words could even form on his lips. Kira looked up just in time to see the vampire jump from the roof. She dove, rolling to the side, aiming her fire. Bull's-eye.

A sickening crunch hit her ears, and Kira turned to see the broken legs of the vampire she had scorched just enough to hurt. Its bones jutted out through charred skin. But still the vamp was clawing through the ground, trying to bite her. Reaching out, Kira finished the job.

There was a pause and Kira's heart fell as she realized what it meant. They were strategizing. Using her mother had failed, attacking from opposite directions seemed futile, and they needed a new game plan.

"Come on!" she yelled. They couldn't stop. She couldn't stop. Already with the pause, Kira became aware of the black tar inching down her veins, leaking from her heart, trying to infiltrate.

She called her flames, circling her heart in Protector powers, trying to fight it off, but the evilness was eating through her defenses. Instead of sensing vampires in the trees, the sweet smell of blood was starting to call out to her. The vampire inside of her was awakening. Her fire was being forced out, was blowing from her fingers at a rapid pace while inside a shadow took its place in her core, trying to block out the sun. Kira pushed against it, calling on her powers, using every bit of will she had not to fall.

But she did fall.

Her knees buckled and she gripped her chest, grasping for the sun with her bare hands. The outside world was slipping away.

But Luke. Her mother. They needed her.

Kira collapsed on her side, keeling over as the internal battle intensified. She didn't see the flames encircling her body, the fire surrounding her entire being. She felt it pulse, felt it melting the tar, turning it to slick oil. Kira pushed harder.

Flames tore free of her skin, escaping into the trees, doing the fighting for Kira. Every few seconds, when her body had had too much, another explosion ripped away, shooting into the world around her. But for the first time, Kira felt like maybe she was running out. Like the cloud was getting thicker, hiding more and more of the sun. Her endless reserves were emptying with each surge that wracked her body.

And then another fire joined hers, flames that were purer, were protecting her—were fighting the darkness for her. And they were winning. They were pushing it back. They were untainted.

They were Luke's.

"Kira, Kira, Kira," she heard. Her senses were returning.

Fingers covered hers, pushing against her heart, forging their own pathway through. Luke. He was saving her. He was fighting the battle she didn't know how to win.

"Luke." She blinked, fighting the desire to reach up and bite his skin, to sink her teeth through his flesh and taste, and taste...

But it was Luke. Her best friend. Her protector. Her rock. Not her food. No matter how good he smelled.

And the thought was so absurd, that the Kira, still conscious, still fighting, gave up and started laughing instead.

"Kira?"

But she couldn't stop, the giggles wove their way around her limbs, shaking her just enough to dislodge the black oil Luke's flames couldn't find, just enough to make it break apart and disappear.

"Okay, you're really freaking me out. We have to go."

Kira blinked again, making out his face against the blue sky, against the red flames silhouetting his features. His eyes were bulging, afraid, desperate. His skin was covered in ash, speckled with black smudges. And then another smell sifted through her nostrils. Smoke. And a heck of a lot of it.

Kira stopped laughing and sat up, slightly dizzy but almost like herself.

The trees were burning.

Kira spun, looking for her mom, who was standing above her holding her hand over her mouth, trapping the sobs that Kira hadn't heard before. And it hit her that the fear in her mother's eyes wasn't from the vampires, it was from her—for her.

Unable to process anymore, Kira looked behind her mother to the house. It was on fire. It was crackling, burning. The dried wood had already turned black, charring in the heat, and gray flames billowed into the sky.

Her house. Her home.

Kira stood up, running toward the door. There were so many things she hadn't looked at. What if she and Luke had missed something? What if there were more clues, more trinkets left behind, waiting for her to find them?

Luke caught her around the waist.

"Kira, we have to go! We have to get out of here."

"But the house, I have to—"

"There's nothing you can do," he said, speaking urgently, trying not to yell. "I have the research, we have to go."

"But—"

Kira was silenced by a loud boom that shook the earth beneath their feet. The tree, the one resting on her house, had fallen through, splitting it down the middle.

It was gone.

A pile of rubble.

Kira screamed but didn't protest when Luke tugged on her hand, running toward a spot in the woods that hadn't caught fire yet.

"Where do we go?" he yelled over the sound of more branches falling to the ground. Her mother had come alive.

"Follow me," she called back to him, pushing through the forest, trying to beat the fire that was hot on their tails.

And hot, oh man was it hot. Hot enough to burn, even if they were conduits. The smolder on her backside was immense, like a furnace had opened behind her. The sting of the heat was unlike anything Kira had felt, but she wondered if maybe it was hurting her more than the others, scorching her in a way it didn't with them.

They jumped through a small stream, and Kira relished the cool droplets that splashed onto her cheeks.

"We're almost there," her mother called back, nearly falling as she turned around to meet Kira's eyes, checking to make sure her daughter was still with them, but in what sense Kira wasn't sure.

And then she saw the clearing up ahead, the bright silver of their car. All three of them sped up, closing the gap quickly, until finally they were all sitting in leather seats, silent except for deep and heavy breathing.

Kira's mother reached for the phone she had left in the car and quickly dialed a number.

"Hello... Yes, I think I need to report a fire... yes, there's a lot of smoke coming through the trees... I don't know what else it could be... I'm driving through the mountains, maybe an hour east of the airport... yes, on that main road... you see it? On the satellite feed?... great, thank you... yes, you too. Have a wonderful day."

She hung up.

More silence.

No one even knew where to begin.

Kira stretched her fingers, bringing her flames just close enough to the surface that she could see the glow under her palms. It was still there. Deep inside, the sun was still there.

She sighed, leaning her head back against the seat to stare at the smoke leaking over the trees and onto the road.

Ominous. That was the only word that came to mind.

"Maybe we should, you know, leave? With the fire and everything, it doesn't seem safe," Kira said while keeping her gaze on the forest. She couldn't see the actual fire yet.

Her mom started the car, slipping away from the curb and making a U-turn on the empty street. They were headed back to the airport.

"So," Kira said quietly, not sure how to finish it. All she knew was she needed a distraction, something to keep the image of her broken home from taking over.

"So," Luke said, taking a deep breath and rubbing his hands against his face. "So you really are turning into a vampire?"

"Yeah," she said quietly, ignoring her mother's concerned gaze, "I think I am."

"Then," he said and reached into his pocket, "we have some reading to do."

"You found something?" Her mom gasped, perking up ever so slightly.

"We did," Kira said and squeezed her fingers.

Luke tapped her head with the bundle of pages, scratching her skin, but Kira didn't take them. Instead, she reclined her seat until it was almost flat and pressed her fingers into her temples. Her head was pounding.

"Can you just read it to us?" she asked.

Luke looked down at her with a smirk, his eyebrow raised.

"Come on, that way my mom can hear."

Kira closed her eyes, not waiting for another sarcastic reaction. But she heard him shift on the leather seats, getting comfortable. Then came the sandpaper like sound of shuffling pages.

"Dear Diary," Luke began, "I think my best friend is trying to kill me."

"Luke," she said wryly, not amused. Except, dang it, a smirk started to pull at her lip.

"Okay, okay." He coughed, getting back into the right mindset and started to hum a little while he scanned for something interesting.

And hum.

And hum.

"Luke," Kira said, trying to lighten her annoyed tone, "a vital part of reading something out loud is, you know, actually reading it out loud."

He sighed. "I'm looking for something new. Right now, he's just talking about the missing pages from that text, the ones we got from your grandfather. It's all Protector and scientific—about the madness, the loss of control—but there's nothing about angels or any of that."

"Humph." Kira crossed her arms, thinking.

"I'd like to hear it," her mother said from the front, keeping her attention on the road.

"Oh, right," Luke said, suddenly alert. He sat up and started reading quoted passages from the text. Kira tuned it out. She'd heard it all before. The Protectors thought their biggest fear was her losing control, her fire turning deadly to humans, her oncoming madness. They didn't even know the half of it—that the madness was the least of their concern. It was what would come after. The killing. The biting. The blood.

Kira rubbed at the spot between her eyes. Better not to think about it, not when there was still some hope left.

"Ooh, this is interesting." Kira perked up while Luke held the paper to her face. "It says 'madness=falling?'"

The scribble was unquoted, unsourced. Just a moment of pure thought from her father. She liked that he used the symbol instead of writing the word equal—it was quick and efficient, getting right to the point.

"What do you think he meant?"

"Well, madness for the Protectors was the moment the fire consumed the mixed breed conduits. When their flames exploded out of them, burning entire villages to the ground, only stopping once they died. At least, that's what the academics thought."

"But falling is completely different," Kira said, thinking out loud. "It's like something takes over inside of me, I can't even feel my fire anymore, there's just this darkness, this smoke that blocks everything else out."

"Maybe to you, but that's not what it looked like to us," her mother said softly. Kira heard her breath shake.

"That's genius, Mrs. D!" Luke exclaimed, shuffling in his seat excitedly. "The madness and the falling, they're the same thing. You practically just burned a forest down, and to us it looked like you were exploding with fire, totally out of control. The madness, get it? But inside, you were really changing, falling."

"That makes sense! It felt like maybe the sun was leaving me, like my powers had run out, but in reality they were being pushed out. The vampire was forcing out the sun, trying to make the change complete." Kira shuddered. How close had she just come to completely crossing over? "But how does this help us?"

Luke bit his lip and looked back down at the papers. "Not sure yet. But we learned something, which is a start."

"Madness," Luke muttered under his breath as he skimmed, "control…fire…burning…killed…" Kira didn't like where this was going. "Here, read this," Luke said and held the pages above her head again.

But what about the healing? Her father had scrawled. *Does it go away or is that the key? Will it save her?*

All questions, no answers.

"What do you think?"

Kira shrugged. "I don't know, it's not something I

really keep track of. Although..." Kira thought back to the fight outside of Sonnyville. Her broken back. Her useless limbs. It had taken a while to heal herself, so long that her mother would have died if not for Pavia. At the time, Kira thought it was just the degree of the injury, but that had never stopped her before.

She thought back further, back to her first visit to Sonnyville. A vampire had flipped their car over, mangled it into pieces and Kira had managed to not only save herself, but also Luke, his sister Vanessa and that girl Casey, who Kira refused to acknowledge as his ex-girlfriend. They all would've died, would have been ripped apart by the car.

In comparison, a broken back seemed miniscule.

Kira looked up, meeting her mother's eyes in the rearview mirror. They quickly flicked back to the road, trying to mask the worry.

"Give me your arm," she said to Luke, looking for a scrape. She flipped his hand over, running her eyes along his forearms until—*aha, there we go*. A nice red cut scarred his elbow.

Shifting in her seat, Kira placed her hand over the spot, letting her mind go blank so she could focus on his skin. *Seal shut*, she thought and pictured the red wound lightening to pink until it disappeared entirely. Her head began to ache, a dull feeling at the crown of her neck.

A few minutes later, when she couldn't concentrate anymore, Kira pulled her hand back. The cut was gone.

Luke looked up, his mind already spinning in circles of what it could mean, of how she could heal herself. But Kira had a different thought entirely—tough. It had been too difficult. Her healing used to come as second nature, without a thought.

"It's going away," she said quietly.

"What are you talking about, going away? It is gone," Luke said, twisting his elbow around to look at the newly repaired spot.

"No, my healing, it's going away. It's getting harder."

His arm dropped. His heart followed. Kira felt the echo in her mind and closed the bond, tightly shutting it.

Nodding toward the paper, Kira asked, "What else does it say? My father's research?"

"Not much." Luke handed her the pages, letting Kira do the reading.

The words were small, the letters straight and slightly slanted to the left. It read like a stream of consciousness, like thoughts pouring from his head. More about the madness, the Protectors, their beliefs. *Of course that's what he would write down*, Kira thought. All of the Punisher culture was in his head, ingrained in his very being.

She flipped over the last page. Nothing new. Nothing she hadn't heard before.

Angels.

Kira stopped, her mind caught by the word she had skimmed over. Backtracking, Kira reread the line.

"The story of the two angels..." she murmured. Searching the page for more information. What story? What angels? But there was nothing, no other mention.

"What'd you say?" Luke asked, looking over her shoulder.

"The story of the two angels," Kira repeated, just as perplexed as before.

"What story?"

Kira rolled her eyes. "I don't know."

Her mother sucked in a breath. Kira head snapped toward the steering wheel.

"I do," her mother said and a smile slowly spread across her face, "I know it."

"Go, Mom!" Kira reached up for the high five and received a resounding slap.

"Sliding in for the win," Luke cheered from the back seat.

It was silent for a moment. Her mom was thinking, trying to drive and bring back an old memory at the same time.

"So, what is it?" Kira asked, impatient.

"Yeah, what is it?" Luke repeated, sounding like a five-year-old.

"It's an old Punisher legend, sort of like a creation story," her mother began. "I don't know why I didn't think of it earlier, although I'm not sure how truthful or helpful it is."

"It's okay." Kira placed a hand above her mother's, letting their fingers intertwine over the clutch. "Anything will help, Mom."

"Do you remember the first Punisher story, the story of how vampires and conduits came to be? Lucifer fell first, bringing other corrupted angels to the earth with him, where they feasted on human blood and turned humans into their own twisted puppets. Seeing this, the pure angels asked God to release them from the heavens so they could bring their brothers back, could save them from themselves, and God agreed. But soon even the pure angels began to change, began to fall. So, to save their souls and the earth itself, they split their powers in half, becoming conduits—beings strong enough to fight the newly created once-human vampires, but not blessed enough to fall into the darkness."

"Right," Kira replied, "that's what the other Punisher told me, back in Aldrich's dungeon. What do two angels have to do with it?"

"Well, within all of this madness, two of the pure angels fell in love."

"It always comes down to a love story," Luke said quietly from the back seat.

"It does," her mom said, smiling sadly into the rearview mirror before turning back to the road, "and like most love stories, this one is star-crossed. The woman had a best friend, a true brother, who had fallen with Lucifer, turning into an evil, mangled original vampire. And the man had a true sister who was killed by his love's brother."

"Jeez, talk about bad luck," Kira muttered under her breath. Why did every story seem to have a sad ending these days?

"But still, the two of them fell in love, and when they realized that the darkness was coming for them, that they would be unable to hold on much longer, an idea came—a way to save each other. They would ask God to strip their divinity, to make them human, so they could live together on earth for however many years a short mortal life allowed. God agreed.

"And when the day came, they held hands, waiting for their powers to be stripped. As the sun leaked from their bodies, however, a thought came to each of them. The woman, still believing her brother was alive somewhere, wished for the power to save him. And the man, wanting more than anything to avenge his sister, wished for the power to end that vampire's life.

"And when God's eternal fire left their bodies, two different people emerged. A Protector and a Punisher. Two races, two flames, and two paths. Knowing what their love would bring, what a child might mean, they went different ways, changing more original angels to their respective causes. And though their love remained strong until they died, the two never saw each other again."

"That is the worst bedtime story ever," Luke said, sighing and leaning back against his seat.

"Tell me about it," her mother remarked, "I used to have nightmares as a child, not dreams."

"But how does it help us?" he asked.

"I'm not sure," her mother said softly.

But Kira had an idea. It was about making a choice. Keep her Punisher powers to kill Aldrich, avenging both her parents and Tristan. Or keep her Protector powers to stay with Luke.

A choice.

Aldrich or Luke.

Her parents or Luke.

Tristan or Luke.

She rolled over, searching the skyline. Smoke. Black clouds still billowed into the air above the trees. All it did was remind her that time was running out. That she needed to choose.

Or a lot more than a forest would burn.

The whole world would crumble.

Chapter Twelve

"There's one thing I don't quite understand," Luke said. The two of them were driving to his house to meet with Tristan and Pavia.

The flight home from West Virginia had been miserable. Kira feigned sleep for most of the ride, unable to sort through her tumultuous thoughts.

Luke picked up his car from the airport parking lot and dropped her mother off at home. Kira wanted to run inside, to hug her little sister and give her father a kiss, but she was supposed to be in Sonnyville, happy and safe. And her facial expression would have given her away, would have made her father know something was wrong. Besides, they had work to do.

There was always more work to do. And the more they drove, the more she worried that Luke saw it too—saw the indecision etched into her features.

Silence filled the car. Luke wanted to read her mind. And Kira, more than anything, wanted to hide that there was still a choice to make, still an unexpected barrier between their futures together.

"What?" Kira asked. Luke had said something, but she had been too deep into her own head to hear him.

"I said, there's one thing I don't quite understand."

"Only one? I'm impressed," Kira mocked, covering up her worry with a smirk.

"Ha. Ha," he drawled. "I meant one thing about the fight. How did the vampires know we were there?"

"Hm." Kira shrugged, unbuckling her seatbelt as Luke's house came into view.

"Don't you think it's strange? That place was totally deserted for years and then on the one day that we're there, a whole troop of vampires is too?"

"Yeah, it's weird," Kira said, pausing while they both stepped out of the car, "but I've seen weirder. One of them probably saw us in the airport or on the road and just followed the car."

"I guess," Luke said, but he squinted one eye, pursing his lips in dissatisfaction.

"Is that music?" Kira asked, straining her ears. It sounded like a violin was playing softly inside of Luke's home. The sound grew as they approached the front door. A soft peel of laughter joined it, followed by a deep muffled voice.

Luke unlocked the door.

Kira's eyebrows drew together. A sharp inhale sucked air into her suddenly burning lungs and an invisible punch knocked her gut, making her stumble backward on unsteady feet.

Tristan and Pavia stood arm in arm in the center of the living room—one hand around her hip, another around his neck, two joined together. He twirled her in a circle. She laughed at her misstep and he smiled, whispering something into her ear. The lights were dimmed. The music romantic. And Kira knew Pavia was anything but clumsy. The first memory Pavia had shared with Kira was of her dancing before a crowd—graceful and smooth.

A brown eye caught Kira's.

Tristan released Pavia, letting her go and stepping a foot backward, away from the vampire's body. He shook his head, confused, looking between the two girls, fighting with two different versions of himself.

Pavia spun, her cheeks puffing into a grin. "Welcome home. Tristan was just showing me how to dance." She placed a hand on his forearm. "And he's a wonderful teacher."

"Funny, I thought you already knew how," Kira replied, hating the jealousy dripping from her voice. This was totally allowed. She had given Tristan up. But even so, the thought of someone else touching him ripped at her heart.

"Not the waltz, silly," Pavia said and stepped back, giggling and sitting on the couch. Maybe Kira was reading too much into the situation.

"How was your visit?" Tristan asked, letting the words come out slowly, carefully, as if he wasn't sure what, if any, line had been crossed.

Kira walked farther into the room, taking the only open seat next to Pavia so both boys had to settle into armchairs. She didn't look at Luke. "Eventful. Any word from your friends?"

"Alessandro should be calling with an update soon, sometime tonight."

Alessandro? Kira silently questioned, before remembering him as Hawk-Nose, the one trying to infiltrate Aldrich's inner-circle.

"We ran into some vampires while we were there," Luke interrupted. "I was just telling Kira how odd it seemed to me."

Pavia shrugged, blowing the ever-straying lock of hair from her forehead, "Maybe. Someone probably just saw you at the airport. Unless you think they followed you all the way from Charleston?"

"No." Luke sighed, letting the word drag out. "If they followed us here from Sonnyville, they probably wouldn't have waited so long to strike."

"What if they followed her mom?"

Kira perked up.

"How would they have known where she was going? It's not like there were tickets they could track. She used the conduit airplane."

"What if they were already listening?" Kira whispered.

"What?" Luke asked. Kira met his eyes, ignoring the quick glance he made between her body and Tristan's.

"What if they were already listening to the conduits? Spying on Sonnyville? The airport is just outside the wall, they could have been watching it." Kira rubbed her temples. A thought was tugging at her, irking her. Something didn't add up.

"But why?" Luke asked.

And suddenly it hit Kira, ramming into her like a truck.

"Of course," she said, squinting and rubbing at her temples. "Why didn't I see it before?"

"What?" Luke and Pavia asked in unison. They didn't see it yet.

"Sonnyville. That's the plan. That's always been the plan." Kira stood and started pacing. "Aldrich, he's going to attack Sonnyville. He knows I won't be able to hideout while all of those people are being attacked. He knows I'll go, knows I'll want to fight him—"

"But you can't, Kira," Luke said, standing too.

"But I have to," Kira said. A choice. It was always about making a choice.

"There are too many conduits—"

"I know."

Luke was right. There were too many conduits. Too many sweetly scented veins to drag her down, to entice her, to push her over the edge. If she went there, used her powers there, she would fall. No questions. That was an absolute. And even more absolute? Conduits would die.

"But I can't let him win."

A choice.

"Hold up," Pavia interjected. "You're saying Aldrich is going to attack Sonnyville? It's suicide."

"He doesn't care anymore," Kira said. "All he cares about is finishing what he started back in England. Turning me. Ending the conduits. God, why didn't I see it before?"

Why didn't she see it when her mother was attacked? Why didn't she realize Sonnyville was always the end goal— always the battleground?

"I need to call Alessandro. Maybe he can confirm it." Pavia stood, retreating to the kitchen.

"I need to call the council. I have to warn them." Luke followed, turning left for the stairs rather than right.

Kira fell back onto the couch, chiding herself. Idiot. It was so obvious. He knew what he had been doing all along. Attacking her mother. Attacking her home. Practically begging her to choose vengeance, to meet him for a final fight. He was never trying to kill her, just to goad her, because he did know. Ever since he had escaped, Aldrich had known that he had been right all along—that she would fall and she would bring the rest of the conduits down with her.

Unless a choice was really all it took. Keep her Punisher powers to kill him, or let them go for the chance at something more.

"Kira?"

She blinked, turning slightly to look at Tristan. What a difference a couple of days could make. His soft chocolate eyes did nothing to lessen her anxiety, but his presence did. The familiarity helped set her mind at ease.

"Yeah, Tristan?"

He stood up, walking over to sit on the edge of the couch, his leg a somehow distant one inch from hers.

"I know I am not the man you remember, but I would still like to help. I can see that you are uneasy, that something more than what's been spoken is troubling you."

"Am I that obvious?" She laughed under her breath.

He shrugged, unsure of how to respond.

Kira took his hand in her lap, holding it between both of hers. "You know what's funny? I mean, not really funny, but strange. You used to be my person, the one who could help me escape when the conduit life seemed overwhelming or my future seemed hopeless. Somehow, you'd distract me enough to make it disappear for a while, to make me feel like a normal teenage girl."

"Maybe I still can," he said, bringing his other hands over hers, so four sets of fingers interlaced.

How? Kira wanted to ask. The old Tristan would talk of their lives together. The places they would travel, the things they would see, the memories they would create. He always avoided serious things, like getting married, since he wasn't legally a person, or having children, since it wasn't possible. But somehow, he managed to talk of the future without making her think of those things. He would make it seem glamorous and hopeful, instead of the truth—that she was completely doomed.

"I'll start by telling you that no matter what happens, you still saved me. I have a feeling that you've saved me once before, during a time I don't remember, but even in the few days that I do, I feel as though I need to thank you."

"No, you don—"

"I do," he interrupted, "you brought me back to life. Literally. You gave me a second chance to be a good person, to get it right. But also in another way. You brought me home, and even though it feels like my parents and brother were alive only a week ago, being here has helped me accept that they are gone."

Gone. They are gone. Why was that concept so difficult to comprehend? To believe?

"Do you miss them?" she asked. This was a new Tristan, one who honored his past rather than kept it from her. In a way, Kira felt like she was getting to know him for the first time, or at least getting to know a side of himself that he had always kept hidden from everyone, even her.

"Yes and no," he said, leaning back in his seat, eyes glazing over. "My mother. I miss her the most. The truly unconditional love she honored me with, it was a rare thing. My father and I, my brother and I—we never really understood each other. I miss them, of course, but not the way you miss a true friend, how losing them feels like losing a part of yourself. I miss them because they were familiar, they were my blood, and there's always something to be said about that. But they were never part of my soul."

"But your mother was?"

"She was everything to me," he said softly, pausing, "and yet, I feel as though another piece of me is missing too, something I don't know how to identify." He looked up at her through the dark black lashes framing his eyes and the slightly shaggy hair that fell down over his forehead. Kira's heart sped.

He was begging her—begging her to tell him what the missing part was. But she couldn't it because Kira didn't know. She didn't know if part of him was dying from missing her, or if part of him was still lost somewhere in the memory of being a vampire. Either way, it would soon be gone, spirited away by Pavia's powers, and he would feel whole again. At least she hoped he would.

"Can I ask you something, Tristan?"

He nodded.

"If you could choose between vengeance and love, what would you pick?"

"Love," he answered quickly.

"Even if it was to avenge your mother? Even then?"

He laughed. "Especially then."

"How are you so sure?"

"All my mother ever wanted was for me to marry, to find a wife, to love. To throw that away would be to disgrace her memory, not to honor it. But perhaps this is a question I should be asking you?" He raised his eyebrows, trying to peer through her, right into the thoughts she was trying to shield. "I didn't quite follow the three of you before, but this man Aldrich, what did he do to you?"

"He killed my mother..." Kira sighed. *He killed you*, she continued in her thoughts. He took away Tristan's soul. He was the catalyst that broke them apart. He was the joker, dancing the dream of her mother around, dangling it like a noose made specially for her. He was the dark hole wedged inside of her heart.

"What do you think she would want for you?" Tristan asked.

Kira thought back to the few memories she had from Pavia. The warm home, the warm thoughts, the big dreams. She knew what her mother would want—for love to prevail. Kira had known what her parents had been fighting for all along—the chance to be happy, the hope that love might just win out in the end.

But another memory pulled at her. Aldrich. Back in England, he had interrupted her in the garden. A dreamer, that's what he called Tristan. But not her. He had named her a realist, someone who worked in facts and not wishes, who lived in the real world instead of the happy fantasy.

Kira didn't know what she was.

There were facts—Aldrich was a bad man, he was attacking Sonnyville, he had to be stopped, Kira could kill him, could choose her Punisher side, but in doing so would lose Luke forever.

Then there were dreams—Tristan finding peace with himself, Kira feeling free of the weight of the world resting on her shoulders, saving vampires who want to be saved, falling in love, knowing the sun would stay with her forever, knowing the killing would finally stop.

A choice.

"Kira."

She looked up toward the staircase where Luke was standing, his eyes glued to Tristan's hands in her lap. His lids closed slowly, painfully, and then he was looking at her, silently pushing any jealousy to the back of his mind.

"I spoke with your grandfather," he said, voice strained. Kira slipped her fingers from Tristan's. He slowly followed suit, hesitating before cutting contact completely.

"What'd he say?"

Luke walked down the stairs before collapsing into his empty chair. "It's not looking great in Sonnyville. The Punishers are still petitioning to have you killed—they think our running away just proved that they had been right. He said they've been noticing an increased vampire presence, and they've turned the UV wall around the town up to a stronger setting. And feelings about you within the town are mixed, and it's hard to tell which side has more support. Basically, gloom and doom as per usual."

"I'm starting to get tired of that," Kira joked.

"Me too."

Kira clicked her tongue, thinking. "Did you tell him about the attack? About our suspicions?"

Luke nodded. She paused, taking a deep breath.

"Did you tell him about me?"

Luke met her eyes, the fire-flaked emerald green pierced through her, and shook his head.

"Are they prepared to fight?"

"As prepared as can be, but he seemed doubtful. If there are as many vampires as we're afraid of, I don't see how the Protectors can fight without any help. The presence of the Punishers will ease the pressure a little, but having me there to strategize and having Pavia's vampires could mean the difference between victory and defeat."

Kira knew where this was going. Me. He had said me—not us. She stood up, pointing at him forcefully and shaking her head. "No way. You are not leaving me behind."

Luke wrinkled his nose and stood to challenge her. "Kira, you can't come. You need to stay away from all of the conduits until we figure out how to stop whatever's happening to you."

"I won't."

"You have to."

"Luke, come on. After all of this? You just want to cut me out? I don't care if you lock me in a closet when the battle starts, but I have to be there. I have to help."

"Kira, it's too dangerous. And not just for you, for everyone."

"I'll just steal your car and drive there. You can't keep me out of this."

"God," he said, and ran a hand through his thick blond hair, sighing, "can't you just listen to me this time?"

"No," Kira said quickly.

"How will you even get inside? Half of Sonnyville wants you dead."

Half? Kira gulped. Her list of allies seemed to be getting shorter on an hourly basis.

"We'll think of something. Zip me inside of your suitcase or something, I don't care. I just need to see my grandfather, to help him plan out the fight. I promise, I'll stay inside, I won't let anyone—not even Aldrich—know I'm there." *Crossed-toes still count right?* Kira thought, wedging her second-toe over the big one inside of her sock. No way would she let someone else fight her fight.

Luke raised his eyebrows. "You'll willingly keep away from the action?" Kira nodded earnestly. Luke snorted. "Please, I've known you too long to believe that one. At least try to be inventive."

Pavia strode in, making no attempt to be quiet as she said goodbye and hung up the phone. *Saved by the vampire,* Kira thought.

"Alessandro just confirmed it. He joined some of Aldrich's cronies and they had very loose lips, good for us. They're amassing outside of Sonnyville, just waiting for the go ahead."

Just waiting for me to arrive, Kira thought.

"Did he learn anything else?" Luke questioned. He flicked his eyes to Kira one more time, letting her know he hadn't forgotten anything.

Pavia shook her head.

"Any word from the other vampires? How fast can you all get there?" Kira asked.

"As soon as you need us, but no sooner. We won't be able to hang around outside of Sonnyville unnoticed. Once we get there, we need to get right to the fighting."

"Sounds good to me," Kira replied. She wanted to end this, once and for all. "Your vamps attack from the outside, Luke and I rally the conduits on the inside and Aldrich is toast."

"I have an idea," Luke said quietly, almost as if he wasn't quite sure he wanted to share it. Kira waited. He tensed and then sat up. "There's another way in, a secret way under the wall."

"Really?" Kira jerked in surprise. Why hadn't he told her?

"It was a backup, in case vampires ever surrounded Sonnyville. A way to get people out if we needed to. But it can also get people in, people like vampires. But only the council knows where it is."

"My grandfather will show us, he—"

"Don't," Pavia said quietly, "don't show us, just in case something happens or someone follows us. We'll fight from the outside, like Kira said."

"You're sure?" Luke asked. "Being inside might provide more protection."

"Or a Punisher might kill us when we're not looking," she replied. Kira sank back in her seat, unable to deny it. If the conduits wanted to kill Kira, nearly one of their own, there was almost no way they would agree to fight peacefully alongside vampires.

All of them stopped talking, choosing to think for a minute instead. Blood rushed in Kira's veins, warming her body, exciting it. The fight was finally here, and this time, Aldrich would not escape. One way or another, he would pay.

"So saying I agree to let you come—"

Kira rolled her eyes and interjected, "Meaning you've realized there's no way to stop me."

"Meaning I'm a kindhearted soul who knows how much this means to you—"

"Who's also afraid of me," Kira supplied.

Luke smirked. "Who's also deathly afraid of pissing

you off—how do we get you inside without Aldrich knowing? We need to hold the fight off for as long as possible."

"We can't drive," Kira said.

"Flights will automatically be suspicious," Pavia said.

"And parachuting is totally out of the question…" Luke deadpanned and looked at her, forcing his wavering lips together. "You might have had something with the luggage."

"For real?" Kira asked, concerned with how serious his voice sounded. He nodded earnestly. Kira couldn't detect a joke…but he had to be kidding, right?

"Not the whole time." Luke sat forward, leaning on his forearms as his features became more animated. "We take the private plane, and when we land, you'll squeeze into a suitcase—don't look at me like that, we can line it with memory foam or something—and then none of the conduits will know you're there. The vampires will only hear my name, hear about me landing, and I can say you stayed with your family, that you're waiting it out in Charleston. I'll go right to your grandfather's house, and we'll open the suitcase there."

"Aldrich won't buy it," Kira said.

"Maybe not forever, but we don't need long. We only need enough time to organize the conduits and give Pavia the final word to attack."

"It might work," Pavia said, shrugging and throwing a

wide, teasing grin in Kira's direction.

A suitcase. Really. Kira breathed deeply. It was for a greater cause, the good of her people...but a suitcase, really?

"Fine," Kira said through gritted teeth, "but you're bringing Tristan with you, Luke." She looked at Pavia quickly, and then to Tristan, who sat up upon hearing his name. Kira had one more thing to do before the fight.

She had to give Tristan his life back. To restore his soul by removing any and all memories of his life as a vampire.

To finally say goodbye.

Chapter Thirteen

She was going to kill Luke...kill him. *I bought the thickest memory foam*, he said. *You'll be fine*, he said. *It'll only be fifteen minutes*, he said.

Kira was going to kill him.

Her entire body ached and she had definitely been in this stupid, dark, suitcase sweating in her own hot breath for at least half an hour.

Ouch.

Another bump. How ridiculously ill paved were the roads in Sonnyville? Kira questioned, wishing she could rub her sore back. When he zipped her up, Kira had sworn that Luke was silently laughing at her with his eyes. But then he had lifted the suitcase to its rollers, so her bottom was wedged painfully in the narrow space taking on her full weight, and Kira knew—this was his grand revenge for never letting him win.

We'll see who's laughing when I finally get out of here, Kira thought, wincing as the car bounced over another pothole.

With no other distraction, she tried to focus on the plan. Pavia had regrouped all of the vampires aside from Alessandro, who was still acting as the inside mole, and they were making their way to the outskirts of Sonnyville—far enough away to avoid Aldrich's detection, but close enough to be there within minutes. And since vamps could usually run even faster than a car, Kira guessed they would be there in an hour or two. Hopefully that would be fast enough.

Luke and Tristan were sitting comfortably inside of the car, hopefully talking loudly about how they had left Kira behind with her mother, how they had foiled Aldrich's plot—just in case there were vampires listening as well as watching. Tristan was pretending to remember everything, and Kira had given him a few key pointers to mention—her falling, the fight in England, how his human body had adjusted to his vampire memories…basically anything that might throw Aldrich off.

And, well, Kira was obviously stuck in the trunk, disguised as a very heavy suitcase filled with books Luke had gathered on conduit lore.

Would Aldrich buy it? Hopefully for the few hours she needed to convince the Protector Council that in order to win this fight, they needed to listen to her.

Ding.

Kira's phone beeped—a signal from Luke that they

were almost there. And sure enough, the car slowed. The suitcase she was in slid forward, banging against the front of the trunk as the tires squealed.

Muffled voices grew louder, and Kira heard the pop of the trunk through the slightly opened zipper to the left of her ear. Holding onto the foam lining as much as possible, Kira braced herself for lift off. Squeezing her body inside of a large suitcase was one thing, but having someone lift it was an entirely different story. She might not be large, but she wasn't a waif either.

Someone moved her, bringing the suitcase back toward the opening of the trunk. Or at least that was the direction Kira thought she was moving, but that could be—

Holy crap, she was airborne. Same as before, her hipbones pushed against the sides of the suitcase as it painfully dug into her skin. And *slam*! Kira's body shook as she was dropped on the pavement. Her teeth bit into her lip, almost drawing blood. Now she was reclining, moving so her back shared the burden of holding her weight, and she was moving, rolling down an uneven path.

Stop. More muffled voices. More movement. Until finally, Kira heard the metal at her ear jingle and zip.

"I'm going to kill him!" were the first words out of her mouth, followed by the quick clamp of her lips to keep the sweet smell of Sonnyville from overwhelming her. *Breathe, just breathe*, Kira repeated to herself, slowly inhaling and exhaling through her nostrils. The darkness wove around her senses, called for the smell of blood drifting through the air, rippled along her canines.

Breathe, Kira said again, calming herself. She kept her powers locked tight. The smell slowly ebbed, getting less and less noticeable. *Control*, she thought. She just had to keep it controlled.

"Who?" Kira was pushed back to reality...to her pained limbs. She stood.

"You!" Kira spun toward the sound of Luke's voice and shoved his chest. "Fifteen minutes? More like an hour! And that foam stuff was crap, I have bruises everywhere."

"I'm sorry," Luke said holding his hands up as if to fend off another attack, but then his eyes sparkled, "but it was your idea in the first place."

Kira's eyes widened and she went in for another shove. "As a joke!"

"I still wouldn't have thought of it if you hadn't put the idea in my head," he said, slipping laughs out between the words and continuing to step backward out of Kira's reach.

She lunged for him anyway.

"Enough," a deep voice boomed behind her. "As much as I side with my granddaughter, there are more important things to discuss. Like why you're even here."

Kira turned around with a sheepish grin. "Hi, Grandpa," she said, waving, and then looked to the side at the smaller but still white-haired woman next to him.

Leaning over to kiss her cheek and offer a light hug, Kira added, "Hi, Grandma."

Luke nodded formally to both of them, regaining his composure, and Tristan reached out for a handshake.

"When I spoke with Luke on the phone, he said you wouldn't be coming."

Yeesh, Kira thought. She had forgotten how down to business he could be.

"I know," she replied, "but there was a slight change of plans. I just, well, there's a lot to fill you in on."

"Tea?" her grandmother asked. Everyone, even Tristan, responded with "yes" and a prolonged sigh. "Why don't we all sit down?"

A few minutes later, five steaming cups were placed on the dining room table, now occupied by Kira, Luke, Tristan, and her grandparents.

"So you think the vampires are gathering outside of our walls for an attack? Led by this man Aldrich? Luke mentioned so much to me over the telephone, which was why we used the UV emitting car to pick you up at the landing strip. But why the secrecy with Kira?"

Luke looked at her, questioning. Kira wasn't sure how much she wanted to reveal.

"We heard the Punishers had gathered strength around here, that a lot of people might not be so welcoming if they saw Kira arrive," Luke said, not lying but not telling the whole story either.

"Is that true?" she asked. He nodded gravely.

"The Punisher Council has done a very good job at making their case, and your running away didn't help things either. A lot of people think that their accusations might be true..." He narrowed his eyes, peering closer at his granddaughter, almost as if he could sense the change in her. And maybe he did, because he was offering her the perfect opportunity to speak up. If she could buck up and take it.

"They are," she said quietly, quickly so she couldn't back down. Staring at her cup, Kira watched the steam rise from her tea in silence, wondering if maybe that was what the smoke inside of her looked like. But hers was dirtier, more like a shadow than steam.

There was a gulp, but Kira couldn't say who it was.

"They are right," she said again, sitting up straight, stopping her cowardly behavior. It was the truth, and she had to keep facing it. "I'm turning into an original vampire, but Luke and I think we found a way to stop it." Or at least she hoped they did, that choosing one power over the other was key.

"How?" her grandmother asked, in her sweet singsong voice that even then seemed somehow happy and hopeful.

"That's not important." Kira paused, not important or just not explainable? *Forget it.* She pushed past the thought. "What matters is that it is happening, I am falling, and

Aldrich knows it. That's why he attacking Sonnyville, in the hopes that I'll fall and bring every other conduit down with me."

Her grandfather met her eyes, transferring some of his strength into her with a meaningful nod. He understood. He knew what was at stake but wouldn't give up. "I assume you have some sort of plan?"

"Of course, sir," Luke leaned forward. "It's unorthodox, but, we made an alliance." He paused to look at Kira. "We made an alliance with vampires."

"What?" Her grandfather's loud voice boomed, reverberating off the walls of the small dining area. Kira reached out, grasping his hand—to comfort him or to hold him in place, she wasn't sure. Her grandmother held his other hand and the two of them locked eyes, almost in an inside joke even though it wasn't the right time for that. Kira held her eye roll back, but her grandmother didn't, and it gave Kira strength—maybe she could change his time-fortified beliefs.

"Just listen." Kira tugged on his wrinkly hand, getting his unsteady attention. "I made an exchange. They'll fight for us, help take down Aldrich, and in return I will turn them human when all of the fighting is over. They know the risks and they want to help."

"I will not willingly allow vampires inside these walls, it's an out—"

"Don't worry," Kira interjected, almost happy Pavia

had had the same thought, "they don't want to come inside. They'll stay beyond the wall, they'll fight from the outside." Kira leaned forward on her thighs as the bigger picture expanded right before her eyes, reminding her what so much of this fight could really be about. More than personal vengeance or vendettas. It could be about a whole new world.

She glanced at Tristan as he silently sipped his tea, listening intently but knowing it was not his place to speak. He was the future. He was the proof that not every vampire was as evil as conduits had always believed.

"Don't you see," Kira continued, "I saved Tristan. And you said it before, we can save more vampires. We don't have to be enemies with all of them. And this fight can be the start of that—the start of Protectors doing what they were always meant to do—Protect. Not kill."

Tristan stared at her from across the table as a small blush rose to his cheeks. He didn't know that, Kira realized. He never knew what his life meant, what his redemption could mean. She crinkled her eyes, letting appreciation light her irises.

Her grandfather pursed his lips, rubbing his palms together. Luke's foot tapped under the table, impatient. This needed to work.

"What's the rest of the plan," her grandfather grunted, giving his unofficial agreement to the first part. Kira smirked and Luke squeezed her thigh reassuringly—so far, so good.

"The rest is business as usual," Luke chimed in, getting excited. "The conduits gather in the town square, ready to face whatever vampires manage to make it over the wall. We form normal ranks and put the children under lock down, guarded with our best fighters and half of the Punisher Council." Her grandfather nodded, but Kira had a slightly different idea.

"Or we evacuate them," she said slowly.

Her grandfather looked at her slowly, eyes widening as understanding took over. "The escape route under the wall."

"That's the one," she agreed happily. "Send them with a protective guard and get them as far away from the fighting as possible."

"Funny you never mentioned that idea before," Luke said under his breath, sensing her ulterior motive.

"It came to me while I was stuffed in the suitcase with nothing but my thoughts to ease my pain," she replied sweetly, a little too sweetly. His eyes narrowed. Dang it, why could Luke read her so well? She couldn't stop now though. "Do we by any chance know where it is?"

His eyes shrunk to tiny slivers.

"Yes, one second…" Her grandfather eased slowly out of his chair, his body betraying the strength his voice evoked. He returned with a large scroll and rolled it out on the table.

Blueprints.

"It starts here, in a hidden passage in the basement, in what has been the house of the head councilman since the day Sonnyville was created."

Kira followed her grandfather's finger as it rubbed against the paper, tracing a thin line that began under this very house, ran straight along the main road, under the wall and emptied right beside the first intersection, at least three miles outside of Sonnyville.

Bingo.

She looked at Tristan. This was his salvation. A way for Pavia to come in, a way for her to erase his memories, a way for Kira to save him from the darkness that haunted his vampiric life.

"What?" Kira asked, shifting her gaze. Someone had asked her a question.

"Is that the whole plan?" her grandfather asked. Kira nodded. "I'm calling an emergency council meeting. Luke, come with me to the town square, tell everyone what you told me over the phone. Do not mention the vampires or the fact that Kira is here, just the imminent attack." Luke nodded, all business.

"Lana, come with us. Lead the children and their guards to the passageway when the time comes, you remember the entrance I showed you long ago?" Her grandmother smiled yes, partly proud of Kira's grandfather for being such a strong leader, but also proud that she could help.

He looked at her. "Kira, stay here and stay hidden. Keep Tristan and yourself out of sight, and whatever happens, do not join in the fight. If what you say is true, and you really are falling, we cannot risk it."

Luke's eyes bored into the side of her head, focusing hard on her response. "I'll do what you say."

Almost, she thought to herself, *almost*.

"Then there is nothing more to discuss. Let's go." He stood up, rolling the parchment paper back into its original tube, before striding from the room. Her grandmother stepped after him, light on her old feet.

Luke turned, but paused, looking back at her. "How much am I going to hate whatever you're planning?"

"Not much," Kira said, her lips popped open, widening of their own accord. She wasn't just saying goodbye to Tristan, she was choosing Luke once and for all. Because she loved him, because he was her best friend, and because she refused to take away Tristan's newfound peace, his second chance at life. "In fact, you'll love it."

Luke brought his eyebrows together, tilting his head and plumping his cheeks to the beginning stages of a grin. Excitement was brewing on the other side of their bond. A sort of hope had sprouted in the corner of his mind but there was also confusion as to what had started it, a sense of doubt. "Then why won't you tell me?"

"I'm waiting for the right time," Kira said, using her fingers to push his chest toward the door. "And two seconds before a big council meeting isn't it. Go." Kira nudged him again, thinking for a second that his indecision was cute, in a totally lovable and easy way.

She kissed him quickly, barely brushed his lips, but still a warm tingle flowed slowly down her body. He leaned down for more, but Kira turned him around and pushed again. Didn't he ever listen? She said it wasn't the right time.

Luke took a second look and ran a hand through his messy yellow locks. Then with a slight shrug, a sign he would let it be, he followed her grandparents out the door.

For a moment, all Kira could appreciate was the fresh air, the clean scent, the almost complete absence of sugar filling her nostrils. The conduits were gone. She had made it through her first interaction in Sonnyville. And she could control it, at least a little, enough to see Luke again before the fight. Because that would be the right time, finally.

Realizing she hadn't moved, Kira peeked out the curtains, following Luke's movement down the block and around the corner.

Go time.

Kira spun. "Tristan?"

"Yes?"

She looked over toward his voice. He was still at the table, sitting quietly and sipping his tea. The black hairs her fingers could trace by memory were in disarray, slipping over his eyes, messy in a way that could only look good. Those lips, ones that had once traced their way down her body, were flushed, hot from the tea. His skin was smooth. His forehead unmarred with concern, despite the chaos that had been surrounding him the past couple of days. And his eyes, brown, but not plain, a rich warm chocolate laced with caramel. She could lose herself in those just as easily as in the deep blue sea that was once in their place.

He would never be her Tristan again. But he was still Tristan, still someone she would always love and could probably love again.

"Kira?" he asked, confused at her prolonged stare.

She had intended to tell him that Pavia would be dropping in, but different words tumbled out. "What do you want to do when you grow up?"

He smiled, tilting his head in surprise. "I'm not certain. I feel like an adult already."

"But you're not," Kira said, sitting back down at the table. "You're only seventeen. Heck, you're younger than me now. You have an entire life ahead of you." And he did. He had an entire human life, a new life not plagued by his past, because he didn't really have one, not a long one anyway.

"I have always loved art, so I suppose something with that."

Kira smiled. "That sounds perfect for you." She looked at him again, imagining age lines along his perfect face, maybe a pair of glasses perched on the rim of his nose. An art history professor, she could see it perfectly. All the girls in his class would come for office hours, gossip about him as soon as they walked out the door. But he would be good at that, history and art. They had always been his favorite things.

"What about you?" he asked.

"A chef, I've always wanted to be a chef." And she could be one, Kira realized, if she could split her powers. If she became a Protector, her life wouldn't be totally ruled by her powers, by vampires chasing her down.

Kira had a choice.

And she realized something she had never thought of before—Tristan deserved one too. He deserved to decide his own fate. She couldn't bear to see that haunting look return to his eyes, to watch him retreat into the recluse he had been before they met—the one who never let anyone get close, never let his walls fall. She loved him too much for that.

But it was his life—his choice.

"Do you want to remember, Tristan?" Kira asked softly, staring down at her fingers rather than at him.

"Yes," he said. Kira sucked in a breath. "And no." She exhaled. "There are things I wish I did remember, things like you, but there are other things too. Watching this entire town prepare for a fight against the thing I used to be, hearing how they attacked you before, how they attacked your mother, it makes me question who I became. And if it was a bad person, who did bad things, I don't think I want to know that that part of me exists."

"You were never a bad person," she said and looked up.

"But I did bad things…"

Kira didn't say anything. There was no denying the truth in that statement.

"I fought in two battles during the Civil War. In the first, I was so frightened that I never fired my weapon. I was saved only by luck. And in the other, I shot a man in the shoulder. I was so overcome with shock that he had time to fire back, wounding me, and I fell. That is my last memory before waking up next to you, and I can live with that. Some might say it was cowardly, but I would rather be named a coward than a killer."

"You're neither," she said gently. "You're a good person." *You opened my eyes to love,* she told herself silently, *you made everything seem somehow possible, and I will always love you for that even if you don't remember it.*

And she would. Even as her love for Luke grew, a small part of her would always belong to Tristan.

Kira pulled out her phone and scrolled down to Pavia's name. She couldn't delay any longer. It was time.

"Hey, Kira. What's up?"

"Where are you guys?"

"Close. We're hanging back until we get word from you. Nothing's started yet, right?"

"No, this is about something else. About something we spoke about earlier, back in Charleston, by the marsh…"

"Oh?"

Kira waited for her to understand. She didn't want to say it out loud, to alert Tristan.

"Oh." Realization dawned. "Oh, that. What about it?"

"We need to do it now, before the fight. I need to know that he'll..." Tristan squinted at her, listening in, and Kira gulped down the words. "That everything will be okay, you know, in case the worst happens."

"The worst being you die or you become an original vampire and kill everyone?"

Kira rolled her eyes and pursed her lips. "Really?"

"Just asking."

Kira felt the smile and shrug through the phone. "Either."

"On a scale from one to ten, ten being you turn into a vampire, what are the chances of me becoming a human after all of this?"

"If you keep teasing me? Eleven."

"All right, all right, ruin my fun. How do you want to do this?"

"Do you remember that secret tunnel Luke mentioned? Its entrance is right out at the end of the road, I'll text you the address. Just follow it until the end, and I'll be there waiting."

"Done," Pavia said, and then paused, holding her breath in a way that made Kira know there was more to say. She waited. "Kira," and there it was, the voice of the Pavia she liked, the honest and caring one, not the shielded, sarcastic one.

"Yeah?"

"You are sure about this right? I mean, once it's done, there's no going back."

Kira looked at Tristan, running her eyes over his face, over the open and waiting expression, the unguarded eyes.

"I'm sure."

"Good, I'll see you soon then."

Click.

It was done.

Chapter Fourteen

Kira paced around the dark cellar, thoughts spinning over the all too many outcomes that the end of this fight could have. But there would be one definite outcome. Tristan would be okay. He would finally feel whole for the first time in over a century.

Now if Pavia would just get here a little faster. Kira had tried calling her, but a secret underground tunnel wasn't really ideal for cell reception.

She scanned the room again. No light bulb and she didn't want to go down the road of using her power, so she strained her ears listening for Pavia's footsteps. But the only footsteps she heard were her own.

Okay stop, Kira told herself and slowed her shuffling feet. Tristan was upstairs reading the history book Kira had given him back in the hospital. Yes, that's right—reading a history book for fun. Sure, he missed out on a few decades of his life, but still. *But that's Tristan,* Kira thought—half-smirking just like he used to do.

A scraping noise started behind her, like stones protesting against one another.

"Pavia?" Kira asked into the void. Who doesn't have a working light in their unfinished basement? Oh right, conduits.

"It's me," a voice said roughly. Oh it was Pavia all right, a slightly ticked off Pavia at that.

"Are you okay?"

"No, thanks for asking. Has anyone be down there in the past, I don't know, hundred years? I'm a walking cobweb." Kira rolled her eyes—Pavia was probably just angry she wouldn't be able to twirl her hair very easily.

"Come on, the lights work upstairs."

"Wait." Pavia reached out her hand, landing it perfectly on Kira's forearm because of her enhanced vision. A few weeks ago, Kira would have jerked away from the touch. But now she really felt like there was nothing to hide—no memory of hers that Pavia hadn't already seen. "Don't you want to hear what's going to happen first?"

"What do you mean?"

"I mean the process of removing his memories."

Kira shrugged. "It's not just like, poof, you don't remember anything?"

Pavia's eyebrow raised, Kira knew it from the tone of her voice. "No, it's not just like poof."

"Oh," Kira said, her body suddenly felt heavy. She turned around, looking for the steps somewhat lit by the crack under the door and sat down. "So what happens?"

"Well, I've only done this a few times before, but those memories have already been in the person's awareness, so I just had to erase them. I can't really explain how, I just make them dissolve into nothingness, just make them fade out. But in order to do that, I need to make Tristan remember. I need to break down the wall."

"So he'll remember everything?" Kira asked softly.

"Yes."

Her hands rose to rub at the spot between her eyes, calming the anxiety that was quickly strengthening.

"For how long?"

"I can't say for sure. I'll work as quickly as I can, but it'll be at least ten or fifteen minutes before the entire process is done."

Ten or fifteen minutes. Ten or fifteen minutes to say goodbye? To kiss? For him to yell? To hate her for ending things between them?

Or would it be worse than just that? Ten or fifteen minutes for one hundred and fifty years of memories? Kira would just be a blip on the radar—one happy thought in the sea of despair that would pour out of him.

She gulped but then nodded. "If that's the only option, then we have to do it."

"Lead the way," Pavia said, so Kira stood and walked

up the stairs, trying to remember that in the end, it would be better for him. It would be worth it.

She noticed Tristan before he did her. Kira couldn't miss the black hair popping over the edge of her grandparent's floral couch. He was right where she had left him—feeling totally safe in her care, totally trusting that Kira would never betray him.

But she couldn't think of it like that. He had said so himself—he didn't want to remember. He wouldn't be able to live with it.

She swallowed.

"Tristan?" His head bobbed, but his eyes were still focused on whatever words he was reading. "Tristan, Pavia is here."

He sat up higher and twisted his head around, following the sound of Kira's voice.

"Good morning," he said, smiling and shutting his book. "I thought you were all staying outside the wall."

"We were," Pavia said, stepping past Kira, farther into the living room. "But I thought of something that might help Kira fight, might help us win." She stepped closer to the couch, looking both innocent and guilty at the same time.

"What?" He stood, looking at Pavia to hear the response. Contact broken, Kira was finally able to step closer, to feel free of the scrutiny that lived only in her head. But she had to stay strong, for him.

"Kira can tell you," Pavia said, nudging her head in Kira's direction. Tristan turned, presenting his back to Pavia, and before Kira even saw her move, white hands gripped Tristan's scalp and his eyes went blank, completely devoid of life. His entire body stopped moving, a puppet with no master. Someone else was in control.

And then a spark.

A hint of something returned.

"Kira?" he said slowly. A lopsided smile stirred on his lips—just wide enough to show he was happy but small enough to hide the fangs that were no longer there.

"Tristan," Kira said, her voice wavering. Was it really him? Was he really back?

He jerked his head forward, but Pavia held it steady, refusing to let him out of her grip. She couldn't lose contact with his skin.

But that didn't stop him. His hands whipped up, gripping Kira's cheeks, pulling her closer, until their lips were molded together. Kira sighed into his touch, letting her hands slide up to grasp his strong shoulders.

He pulled her back, eyes wide and grin even wider. "You saved me, you turned me human, oh god, how did you, for days I've just wanted to tell you how much I love you."

He tugged again, bringing their mouths back together, forceful, like a drowning man who needed water. Kira obliged. It was the last time this would ever happen after all, the last time Tristan would remember all of the nights Kira would never be able to forget.

"How do I remember?" he asked with a voice colored by wonderment. "How did I ever forget?"

He stroked her cheek, lightly running his thumb from her lips all the way to the base of her earlobes—strips of skin that remembered his touch. His eyes drank her in, scanning every inch of her body, remembering it as belonging to him. Kira leaned into his palm, trying not to let the brimming tears fall down her cheeks.

He brought her close again, this time kissing every inch of her that he could—quick pecks landing on her nose, her chin, her forehead, any wisp of open skin he could find. And then he started laughing. Tears did start falling, but they were ones of happiness. And Kira let hers out, a mix of joy and sadness, selfish love and selfless love. Now that he was back, she wanted him to stay, wanted to rip him from Pavia's hands and end it.

She put her palm over his, holding his warm skin to her cheeks, drinking him in through watery eyes. Oh god, she had missed him.

But then Tristan stilled.

Kira's heart stopped. Was it already over? She never said goodbye.

His grin retreated. His lips closed, pressing tightly together. The light in his eyes faded, turning dark. The chocolate clouded over, like a shadow had fallen. His knees wobbled, so did his eyebrows. The hands on her face began to tremble—a shake that traveled up his arms until his entire body was vibrating.

"Tristan?" Kira asked.

His palms slid from her cheeks, landing lifeless at his sides.

Kira looked at Pavia. The vampire was staring straight ahead, looking beyond Kira into something otherworldly. She was reliving everything with Tristan, inside his mind, working through it. What was going on?

Tristan's lips fell open. His eyes widened, viewing some horror Kira didn't understand.

In the same moment, his knees gave out, his hands shot up, gripping the back of his neck, and a wail erupted from his entire body. A scream that didn't sound human, didn't sound possible, as though his body were being ripped apart, or maybe it was his soul shredding to pieces.

Tristan fell.

Pavia, still holding onto his head, dropped too, and Kira followed, pulled down by her heartstrings.

She hugged him, trying to control the shakes wracking his body, but nothing worked. The cry had stopped, leaving only silence, but it was almost worse, an absence not only of sound but also of the man.

His eyes rolled into the back of his head, leaving only whiteness visible. His limbs jerked left then right, shifting up only to slam down to the ground. Kira was flung to the side as his body continued to twitch uncontrollably.

Another scream pierced her ears, tearing his vocal chords with its strength. It puttered out into a whimper, then a panting breath, and then words.

"No, no, no," he repeated, in a low voice, a barely there whisper. "What am I, no, stop, no, don't, I can't," Tristan continued, his voice getting louder. His left hand balled into a fist, slamming into the ground over and over with each word, bloodying his skin and the wood beneath it.

"Tristan." Kira reached out, tried to touch him, to comfort him. She couldn't watch him fall apart anymore. She knew what was coming, what would happen if he remembered, but watching him break right before her eyes was too much.

She touched his hot skin, burning flesh that felt as though a fever had quickly spread along his body. Her fingers were rejected. He twisted away from her touch, staring at her as if she was someone else, someone he refused to look at let alone touch.

"I'm sorry," he said, his body still jerking. "Oh god, I'm sorry, I didn't mean, I can't control it, you just..." He crumbled again, hugging his knees into his chest, rocking slowly back and forth on the ground whispering apologies and refusals over and over again.

His skin was whiter, more ghostly than when he had been a vampire. His eyes had come back, but they were trapped, stuck open and staring at a scene Kira wished she could understand just so she could help him in some way.

And then his body stopped, his limbs fell open on the ground, unmoving, and his breath became shallow. Pavia had been right—no human could survive remembering the emptiness that came from being a vampire. No human could live with the soullessness, the horror, especially not Tristan, the artist, the believer.

He was dying, dying from remembering everything about his life.

But Kira refused to let that happen.

She jumped forward, placing her hands over his heart, on the firm chest she used to fall asleep on. Her powers surged, but Kira willed them away, refusing to let the darkness confuse her thoughts. Instead, Kira pumped her hands, pressing on his chest.

She leaned down, sealing her warm lips against his cold ones, and for the first time, the fact that his lips were cold frightened Kira. Because they weren't the cold lips of a vampire, they were the cold lips of death.

She forced air into his still lungs. Pumping one, two, three. Breathing. Pumping. Breathing.

Beat, damn you, Kira thought, refusing to cry, because crying would mean that he was lost. *Just start beating*, she repeated again and again, *just stay alive a little while longer.*

And almost as if he heard her prayers, Tristan's lips opened and he gasped, sucking air into his body. His heart sped, getting stronger, slowly regaining a life of its own.

Kira pulled back as his eyes fluttered open. He sat up—dazed, confused—and looked around.

"What's going on?" he asked. Still her Tristan, Kira sighed, recognizing the tone in that question. She reached over, stroking his cheek while a small, sad smile spread across her features. It was time to say goodbye. "It feels like I was dreaming, like I'm waking up and everything else is slowly fading away."

He touched his forehead, squeezing his eyes tightly shut and then opening them again. "Kira?"

Her hands fell to his lap, holding tightly onto his fingers.

"Tristan," she said, sighing. "I'm going to miss you more than you'll ever know." And he wouldn't know, his memories would be gone, but Kira would keep them close to her heart, alive enough for the both of them.

"You're doing this aren't you? I mean, it was your idea?"

Kira nodded, hoping he would understand. For a moment, pain danced across his features, but then it softened and he broke free of her grip to run his fingers lightly along her jaw line.

"You're always trying to save me," he said, letting a lopsided grin takeover.

"You won't need to be saved anymore," she told him softly, bittersweetly.

"You saved me the moment you let me love you, let

me know that some part of me was still capable of being good."

"You didn't need me to be a good person," she said, shaking her head. He had always been that way, been gentle and kind, at least to her.

"But I did. You brought me back to life, more than once." He stopped, shaking his head, trying to pull at a fading memory. "How did we meet? Will you tell me again?"

A sob pulled on the back of her throat. It had begun. Her voice was shaking. "At school. In our English class."

He laughed. "That's right. Then what happened? Did we go to the marsh?"

Kira closed her eyes slowly, taking a deep breath. She couldn't do this. So instead, she leaned down, putting her head on his shoulder, the little nook next to his neck. Tristan wrapped his arms around her, holding her close.

Kira listened to his beating heart, his beating, human heart. She did that. She saved him. She'd brought him back to life.

Tristan lightly pushed her back, made her sit up, and gripped her shoulder strongly. His eyes were clear, focused, like he understood everything that was going on—as if his entire life were flashing right before his eyes in the moment before it disappeared entirely. And maybe it was.

"I love you," he said, his voice steadfast.

"I love you too," Kira told him, trying to equal his resolve, but her voice was cracking. He was dying right before her eyes. The Tristan she knew, the one she loved, was almost gone forever.

He gripped her face, running his eyes over the curve of her lips, her lashes, her cheeks. He wiped away the tear she couldn't contain, kissing it away, and then leaned down to gently kiss her lips one last time. It was salty, but perfect.

He pulled back. Kira couldn't move. The resolve was vanishing, the light, the memories. Kira watched them flash and fade.

"Thank you," Tristan whispered, and then his eyes closed and he fell, as if in slow motion, back to the ground, curled on his side like a sleeping child. A small smile curved his lips, and his face looked relaxed, perfectly at peace.

Kira was the opposite. Her hand covered her mouth, holding back the crying sounds she wanted to make. Her tears fell silently. Her body shook.

Pavia, job done, let Tristan go. She stepped over his body and wrapped her arms around Kira.

And though she was cold, and technically Kira's enemy, it didn't matter. Kira hugged her back, crying into her shoulder, getting comfort from the woman who had somehow become her friend.

"He's gone," Kira cried. Tristan, her Tristan, was just a memory living inside of her head.

"He's alive, Kira, he's right there, breathing, because of you."

Kira looked over Pavia's shoulder at Tristan.

"He's in a better place now," Pavia whispered, continuing to hug her tightly. "You saved his soul, you saved him."

She heard Pavia. She knew the words were true, but it didn't ease the pain.

Kira leaned back, letting her go. The only person who could truly make her feel better at that moment was Luke, who was still in the town square, hopefully convincing everyone that a fight was fast approaching.

A fight that wouldn't stop just to let Kira ease her wounded heart.

She sniffled, drawing the tears back in. "You have to leave," Kira said, "you have to leave, and you have to bring Tristan with you. I'm trusting you to keep him safe."

"Wouldn't it be better to leave him with you? Inside the wall?"

Kira shook her head, reality crashing back down. "I don't know what's going to happen to me, if I'll even be able to keep it together. If vampires find a way in, come looking for me, I won't be able to keep him safe. I can't use my powers, not to fight." The shadows were too close.

Pavia looked down, her features soft—her hard, sarcastic exterior had evaporated. "I won't let you down."

They both knelt, leaning over Tristan's body. Kira brushed a strand of ebony hair from his face, looking at him one last time with love in her eyes.

Pavia reached out, but Kira stopped her with a touch.

"You told me once that vampires couldn't love..." Kira trailed off.

"I was wrong," Pavia said.

"But it's why you want to turn, right? For that chance?"

Pavia nodded slowly, wondering where Kira was going.

"Could you love him?" Kira asked, her voice barely above a whisper, her fingers still gently stroking his cheek.

"Not as I am now," Pavia said. Kira shifted to look into the vampire's clear blue eyes. "But the girl I once was, the one I want to be again, I think she could. I can see her falling head over heels for a guy like him."

Kira nodded. There was nothing else to say. And Pavia understood. She reached under Tristan's body, lifting him easily from the ground. Kira stayed seated, glued to her spot as Pavia turned and walked away, disappearing into the basement.

Stones scraped, shuffled below her, and then Kira was alone. Pavia and Tristan were gone, escaping through the tunnel, running with vampiric speed out of Sonnyville.

Kira curled into a ball, slipping over onto her side. She dreamt that his arms were around her, cradling her, rocking her back and forth to soothe the pain. She didn't think it would be this hard to say goodbye. But it was. It was hard remembering everything that Tristan had just forgotten.

The first time they met, she fell right then. Looking at him, meeting those crisp blue eyes seconds before class began, it had been enough. That afternoon in Charleston he had been a puzzle she couldn't wait to solve, a challenge that hooked her interest. Even when she had realized what the secret was, that he was a vampire, she hadn't been able to stay away. The day in the marsh was still perfect, something no one could take away.

The memories played one by one, making her smile, laugh, cry some more, until finally her thoughts reached England. Her chin shook remembering the night they had shared, when Tristan was the happiest she had ever seen, when he believed the future was theirs for the taking, that the two of them could be together forever.

But Kira had always known differently—they were doomed from the start. But, she smiled, Kira wouldn't have changed a thing, not even today, not even the end. He was at peace. The haunt to his eyes, the walls Kira had always wanted to bring down, they were finally gone. His soul was healed, and if that meant he had to forget, Kira would remember their happiness enough for the both of them.

And that thought made her sit up, because this wasn't the girl Tristan had fallen in love with. It wasn't who he would want her to be. More than anything, Tristan wanted Kira to be happy, to be the fighter, the spark of life.

Kira rubbed the tears from her eyes, drying them, and stood, taking a deep breath to steady herself.

The day wasn't over yet.

But one thing was. She had made her choice—it was Luke, it had to be Luke. Her parents would have wanted her to choose love, and even Tristan would have wanted her to choose happiness, to live her life. So she would try to let her Punisher powers go, to release them, to split herself to save herself.

To choose love.

To choose Luke.

But just in case, Kira had always known what the backup plan would be. She would rather die than fall, would rather have her friends mourn than fear her. If the price to keep the conduits alive was death, Kira would do it, because she was strong, and because she refused to be the killer Aldrich wanted her to be.

That was her vengeance.

Kira walked slowly over to the suitcase resting in the corner of the room and slipped open a zipper. A small pocketknife fell out, the one she knew Luke kept in his bedside table. It had been a gift from his father when he turned of age, when he went on his first mission.

And Kira had stolen it to do something Luke would never ever agree with.

She flipped open the blade, feeling along its edge. Razor sharp.

If she couldn't split her powers, couldn't transform into a true conduit, couldn't stop herself from falling, there was another option. It wasn't just turning into a conduit or falling into an original vampire. There was death too—a third choice that only Kira and the Punisher Council had been willing to admit existed.

Kira flipped the pocketknife shut, stuffing it into her sneaker, wedging it somewhat painfully beside her foot.

Just in case, Kira told herself, she needed it just in case.

But then her heart lifted.

Luke was close, Kira could feel him, could feel the excitement bouncing off of him in waves. The council meeting must have gone well, his thoughts were bubbling over the bond, but Kira let them come, let them flood her senses and overwhelm her—a river of champagne.

Instantly, her mood began to shift. Happiness tingled down her arms, her legs, up her spine into her very thoughts.

Kira began to laugh, because the closer he came, the closer he was to knowing that Kira had made her choice, and he was it.

Kira raced to the door, peering out the glass to wait and watch for his blond head to appear around the corner.

Luke, she said to herself. She was in love with him and finally, finally, Kira could tell him how she felt—how she might have felt all along.

Luke, she sighed, letting his name send a sense of calm around her body.

Luke, she repeated, forcing the slight pain of the knife in her shoe out of her mind.

He was here.

Chapter Fifteen

As soon as Luke opened the door, Kira jumped on him—arms thrown around his neck, lips landing tightly on his.

Instinctively, Luke caught her around the waist, securing her with his lean but strong arms. Without question, he returned her kiss, moving his mouth naturally against hers, as though the two belonged to each other.

He stepped farther inside, bringing Kira with him, but she didn't notice. Her thoughts were completely consumed by Luke. Making her choice, finally knowing once and for all that Luke was her future, had awakened something within Kira. Her inhibitions were gone—any urge to stop, to hesitate, had vanished.

Instead, she ripped apart the wall she had built in her mind, letting Luke fill every part of her, mirroring every one of his emotions with her own.

I love you, she thought, and hugged him tighter, forcing

the thought with her actions because she didn't want to break for words.

But Luke pushed against her hips, gripping them with his hands, and pulled her toward the far away floor. Kira lifted her feet. She didn't want to stop. But Luke pressed, leaning his head back to break their contact.

Kira dropped her hands, slipping slowly down his body until her feet landed silently on the floor. Their breath mingled in the small space between their lips, heavy and ragged. Kira looked up into Luke's quizzical eyes.

"Kira?"

She nodded. He continued breathing heavily, trying to regain some brainpower.

"Do you know why I stopped us?" he asked, brows furrowed together in true confusion.

Kira shook her head—she didn't feel like talking. He shrugged.

"Me neither." He lifted her back up, pulling Kira into his chest to seal their lips together again. She smiled against his mouth, grinning wildly, as he walked both of them to the couch.

He half-sat, half-fell and Kira landed on top of him, straddling his hips, actually taller than him for once.

Luke pushed her back. "I remember," he panted.

Kira leaned forward, trapping his lips. She didn't care.

"It's." Kira kissed him. "About." She interrupted him again. "The council."

Kira paused, but Luke's fingers were reaching under the hem of her shirt, skimming the bare skin above her shorts and she couldn't think of a response. There was a battle raging inside of his head. She blocked it out. Her resolve was very much fixed in one direction, and for once it wasn't business.

His palms landed on her shoulders, pushing her back. "Okay," he said, trying to be firm, but his voice was airy. Kira met his eyes—his sparking, dancing eyes. She traced the line down his freckled nose, following the slight curve to the left side of his lips. Her fingers inched up, twirling a lock of blond hair between her fingers.

Her gaze traveled back to his eyes. His resistance was adorable.

"I love you," Kira said, her voice strong and steady, despite the lack of oxygen in her lungs.

Luke groaned, reaching for her again. He cupped her cheeks, bringing Kira close, and reached his fingers back around to the base of her neck, gripping her hair.

Then in one swift move, Luke pushed Kira onto the other sofa cushion and stood up, completely separating their bodies.

Panting and pacing, he started to speak, low at first and then louder. "No, there is an imminent battle outside. A whole town of conduits depending on us, not to mention a whole troop of children heading this way. We can't, I mean, that was awesome, amazing, not that I'm complaining, although I guess technically this is complaining, and now I'm mumbling..." He stopped, finally turning in Kira's direction, where she sat innocently with her hands crossed. "What in the world has gotten into you?"

Kira smirked. Where there had been pain associated with the words before, there was now only excitement. "Pavia erased Tristan's memories."

"How did she..." He shook his head, a grin slowly spreading. "Wait, he doesn't remember anything?"

"No," Kira said. "I told her to erase all of the memories of his life as a vampire. All of them."

"Why?" he said cautiously. Hope glimmered in his fiery eyes.

There were a few reasons, she knew there were, but in that moment Kira could only think of one. "You."

Luke closed the gap, kissing her again, before quickly pulling away. He shook his head, clearing his glazed-over eyes. "God, you are driving me crazy right now."

"Don't I always drive you crazy?" she asked sweetly.

"In more ways than one," he said wryly.

Kira stood and Luke took a step back. She walked forward. He veered around the other side of the couch, using it as a barrier, and pointed at her. "You, stay back."

Kira rolled her eyes and shuffled her feet forward.

"Kira, I'm serious. We have a lot to figure out." He didn't sound very serious. In fact, he sounded a little torn. She lifted her foot...

"Obi-Wan never had to deal with this," Luke mumbled and shifted backward.

Kira sighed and crossed her arms. "Fine, go ahead."

"Okay." He nodded and looked around, grabbing a chair from the dining room. "You sit on the couch," he said, jerking his head in that direction. Once Kira obliged, he set the chair down a good five feet away and sat.

"So, what do you need to tell me?"

"Aldrich started his attack."

A cold pitcher of water landed on Kira's head, breaking the trance that had fallen over her body. The battle was here. "Why didn't you say that earlier?" she demanded.

Luke's entire body slackened and he raised his eyebrows in disbelief. "I can't win with you," he whispered to himself after a minute.

"Nope," Kira teased. "What's going on out there?"

"It was actually pretty great timing." He leaned forward, resting his tan forearms on his knees. "Your grandfather was trying to convince the Punisher Council and the entire town that an attack was coming, but there was a bit of resistance. Even after last time, people think Sonnyville is impenetrable. And right as he was about to lose the crowd entirely, one of the Protectors he sent to guard the gate came running up, screaming about the hoard of vampires outside. After that, everyone shut up and started paying attention."

Kira ran a hand through her hair, getting stuck in the

tangled curls. "Have any vamps made it inside?"

Luke shook his head. "Not yet, but I suspect with so many they'll be able to figure something out eventually."

She nodded her agreement. "What's the plan? What did the council decide?"

"A first line of defense has been deployed. Protectors armed with swords and half of the Punisher Council set up base at different intervals along the wall to watch for any vampires breaking through and to start burning any vampires who get close. All of our security cameras have been turned on and we have a team monitoring them. The other conduits have been divided into squads, waiting for words about where they're needed."

"So, not like last time with that whole circle set up in the town square?" Kira asked, thinking back to the other time she had witnessed an attack on Sonnyville. Half of the conduits would have died if she hadn't been there to put an end to the group of vampires that had managed to jump over the wall.

"No," Luke said, a glint in his eye, "this time we're ready. This time, the vamps won't have it so easy. The UV wall is fully amped up, and it'll take them a while to figure out how to get through. And hopefully a Punisher will be there to burn them before they even touch Sonnyville soil."

"Good," Kira snorted. "What about you? What will you be doing?"

A sense of concern tickled at her chest, but Kira tried

to quiet it. Luke could handle himself. He would be fine.

"Well, first I was supposed to check in with you and Tristan…hey, where is Tristan? And actually, back to that, how did Pavia get inside?"

Kira bit her lip. "I might have told her to use the top secret tunnel connected to this basement."

"Kira," Luke gasped, "did anyone see her? Was she followed?"

"Relax." She wished she could reach out and comfort him. "Do you see any vampires around? No one saw her. And I told her to take Tristan with her, to keep him safe since I…" She trailed off, looking at the ground. *Since I can't*, she finished the thought silently.

Luke misunderstood. "Don't tell me you're going to go hunting for Aldrich? Kira—"

"I'm not," she interjected, quickly cutting him off and smiling. "I love you, you idiot, I'm not going to throw that away. I won't give Aldrich the satisfaction."

"You know, you could have ended that like, I love you Luke—I would never make you worry like that. Or, I would never do that to you."

"Or you could just smile sweetly and say, thank you. I love you too, Kira." She raised an eyebrow, letting a little diva attitude flow into her face.

"Thank you. I love you too, Kira." He pursed his lips, holding in a Cheshire-cat-sized smirk.

"I would shove you if I could."

"Too bad your arms aren't long enough."

"Too bad you needed to sit five feet away to fend off my advances."

Luke opened his mouth, then shut it quickly.

"Ha!" Kira perked up. "Gotcha."

"You know I really do love you, don't you?" he asked, tone turning just serious enough for Kira to sense his earnestness.

"I really do."

"Good, because I need to go lock you in a closet."

"What?" If she had been drinking water, it would be all over Luke's lap at the moment. "You don't trust me to stay put?"

"Trust is such a harsh word," he said slowly.

"Harsh and accurate."

"Do you even trust you right now?" he asked, wincing while he did. But Kira didn't want to hurt him, and more importantly, she couldn't deny it. The shadows were there, swirling, strengthening even just in his presence. Being locked up for the duration of the battle might not be such a bad idea.

"You're right." Kira sighed. "Let's do it."

"Good, because—"

But Kira didn't need to hear the end of Luke's sentence, couldn't if she even wanted to. The banter had ended. The professions of love had ended. The moment for kissing was long gone, or maybe it had gone on too long.

Her gut punched inward, hit by some invisible force, and Kira doubled over.

Luke had mentioned it earlier, but Kira hadn't been paying attention, she wasn't listening. She couldn't ignore it now.

The children were coming.

Their innocence, their sweet, succulent innocence—it hit Kira like a wall, slamming through her senses, blocking out everything but smell.

Her canines began to ache. Saliva gathered, pooling beneath her tongue. The need to taste it was overpowering, was undeniable.

The darkness swirled into her vision, creating spots in her eyes, so all she could focus on was the desire slivering down her throat, encasing her heart. The shadows awakened, and Kira shivered from the cold traveling to her limbs. The vampire inside of her was coming out.

No.

No.

Kira dropped to the floor, slamming her fists into the ground as she landed. There was no way this was happening, not now, not when she had finally chosen a path, a dream, a life.

Fire warmed her fingers, traveling in from the outside, spreading warmth to her dying body.

Luke. It had to be.

Kira welcomed his pure, untainted flames, and pulled

them into her, cracking the shadows around her heart so the Protector powers could flood her core, urging her hiding fire awake.

Kira squeezed the fingers wrapped around hers.

"Get me out of here," she gasped.

Arms scooped her up, lifting her high into the air. Kira let Luke carry her away, anywhere other than the floor, right next to the crack under the door where that scent was pouring through.

They moved farther away. The thud of Luke's steps was all Kira could process. Her mind was easing just a little as his fire continued to charge in. Apprehension flooded her thoughts, spilling over the wall. Luke was scared—not for himself, but for her.

Kira's bottom touched a cushion, sinking into a seat somewhere else in the house.

"I'll be right back," Luke urged. His flames retreated, pulling away, and Kira's body went on overdrive. Her own powers tried to push out, pressing against her skin as though a bomb was about to explode, but she held on. She couldn't release it. She would burn the entire town down—because Kira knew deep down her powers were being pushed out, being forced out, and she refused to let them go.

Luke's burning fingers touched her skin again, sending peace and calm to her senses, spreading a golden warmth that had nothing to do with blood, just with fire, pure and untainted fire.

Something pushed against her nose, but Kira turned away. She couldn't open those senses again, couldn't breathe through anything but the slight opening of her lips, the barest hole to let airflow stiffly in and out.

"Kira, just smell it," Luke soothed, running one flaming hand up and down her arm.

Trusting him, she did what he said, reopening the path to her nose.

A putrid floral scent infiltrated, stinging its way down the back of her throat, itching her tonsils.

Kira shook her head, but Luke held it steady, not letting her escape. She breathed the acid flowers in again, hating the fake sweetness, the faux-rose. She couldn't, she wanted the sugar, the real honey, the blood.

Kira coughed. Her entire body, doubled over, jerking with the force of the air expelled from her system.

She coughed again, a long series ending in a should-be-blinding sneeze.

But it wasn't blinding—the shadows had already stolen her sight. The sneeze jostled the darkness, shifting it ever so slightly, but just enough that the hint of a spark poked through.

Kira blinked. Rapidly shifting her eyes, she forced away the black blocking her vision, willed away the spots until the sight of flames seeped through. A wall of orange and yellow rose up, swirling around her face, sinking into her skin. She turned a notch, finding the matching fire in

Luke's eyes. It was his power, not hers. His fire was saving her.

Another breath.

Kira held on tight to the flames swirling in those steadfast irises. Luke wasn't letting her go anywhere he couldn't follow. Like always, he was there, dragging her back to life.

Another breath.

Her heart was slowing, matching his calm pace. Her fire was settling back into her system, following the path Luke's had created, relaxing and retreating back into her core.

The shadows were there, but they weren't consuming her.

Fake flowers still tickled her nose, and she resisted the urge to cough again.

"What is that?" Kira whispered.

Luke shrugged, pulling the bottle out from underneath her nose. The sweet sugar of blood drifted back in, but Kira was in control, and she pushed it as far away as possible, focusing on the tiny bottle in Luke's fingers. It looked like perfume.

"Eau de grandmother," he told her, then winked. "Works every time."

"Well, it worked this time anyway." Kira sighed and sat up, stretching her back. The scent of blood was slowly getting stronger, was calling her back.

"Luke, I have to get out of this house before the children get here."

"They'll be here any second," Luke said, looking over his shoulder and out the window to the front yard.

"It doesn't matter, anywhere is better than here."

Luke turned back around, meeting her eyes with a worried frown. Something was on his mind, something not about her. Kira sifted through his feelings, working her way around his mind. There was love, a passionate love focused on her, and a little something else. A love without lust, a love completely disconnected from her, an innocent one, a long-shared devotion.

"Your brother," Kira said slowly, realization dawning. "TJ is with the kids isn't he?"

Luke nodded, his brows furrowing deeper. "I just want to see him leave, want to make sure he gets evacuated properly. I know TJ, and I doubt he'll go without a big shove from me. He wants to be the hero, you know, the one from his stories."

He wants to be his big brother, Kira thought silently, and brought her palm up to his cheek. She could do this for him, she would make it, she would give him one less person to worry about.

"Then let's stay, with your help I know I can do it," Kira said and squeezed his arm reassuringly.

Maple syrup dipped into her senses—the blood. It was getting stronger.

"Kira, they're almost here." Luke pulled her in close, wrapping his arms around her, bringing his flames back to life again.

Kira ducked her head into the nook below his neck, concentrating on his hot skin against hers. She cut off the connection to her nose, trying her best not to smell him, not to give in to temptation. Luke kissed her forehead, bringing his power to full strength at the same time a fresh round of innocent, untainted blood rushed through her senses.

Kira rocked in Luke's arms, listening to his fire crackle around her.

The door creaked downstairs.

Kira gulped, swallowing down a long batch of air before clamping her lips shut and holding her breath. Lifting her hands, she covered her nose, shutting the world out entirely.

"Luke? Kira?" The singsong voice of her grandmother called.

"Keep everyone downstairs," Luke yelled back roughly.

Silence was the only response they received, silence and the faster shuffle of tiny stomping feet.

Her fingers trembled against her mouth. Her throat burned from lack of oxygen. Her arms twitched, body shaking, rejecting her plan. Spots invaded her vision.

Unable to take it any longer, Kira's entire body lurched and her lips shot open, drawing in a ragged breath.

Sugar. Lollipops and gumdrops. The deliciousness of pure innocence. Nothing would be so wonderful to drain.

Moving without thinking, Kira pushed against Luke's hug, fought his hold. She needed to get out, to be free, to give in, to drink.

Luke's hand slapped her chest, injecting his flames directly into her heart. A jolt of adrenaline racked her body and Luke pushed his thoughts full force into Kira's mind. She was drowning in them, in the strength and loyalty—in the love. Drowning in a way she welcomed, because the alternative was falling, was ripping free of his arms and leaving him.

Hold on, his thoughts told her.

I love you, they said.

His fire was a warm hug, touching every part of her body and soul, so pure and so true that the shadows could do nothing but retreat, but run far away.

"Come back to me, Kira," he whispered, in a soothing voice that slowly pulled her free of him, slowly brought her back.

"Kira," he quietly said again, hugging her close and kissing her forehead, keeping it securely nestled against his shoulder.

Hesitant, scared, Kira let her nose open, let the air around drift in.

It was clear. Clean almost. She smelled the faint scent of Luke's conduit blood, but she could control that urge.

She sat up. She had made it. They had made it.

Kira turned, excited, but Luke was only half there, his eyes were only half focused on her.

"The children, they're gone, right? They made it out?" Kira asked, her thoughts running quickly, trying to understand.

"They're gone," he said, patting her arm. "But..."

"But what?"

His lips wavered, struggling with the question of what to do.

"Luke, tell me."

"It's TJ." He bit his lip. "I didn't see him with the other kids."

Kira's eyes widened. How was this happening? He had to go, he had to find his brother, but... her mind slowed, selfish, but he couldn't leave her alone. Could she even do this without him?

"I'm sure he's fine," Luke said, but Kira heard the doubt pull at his words. "He's probably with my parents."

But what if he's not? Kira heard the unspoken question.

She stood, slipping from Luke's lap, giving him a way out.

"Go," she said. "Go find your brother. I'll stay here. I'll be fine." Even as she said the words, the distance from Luke's body made the shadows grow.

"Kira," he said slowly.

"Luke, I mean it, that was the worst of it. I'm not

going to go looking for Aldrich, and I won't leave this house. The children are gone, the rest of the conduits are out fighting. I can control myself, I promise. Go find your brother."

"He's probably with my parents—"

"But what if he's not? What if he's doing exactly what you told him not to—walking around out there, looking for a real life vampire like in his stories?" She hated to do it, but Kira refused to be babysat. She loved Luke. She wouldn't sit by and hold him back from doing what he did best, rescuing people. This was a fight she would need to end by herself.

Luke sighed. A battle raged in his eyes.

"You sure you'll be okay?" he asked, a guilty look crossed his features as he looked at her.

Kira gripped his cheeks, forcing him to look at her. "I promise. I'll be right here waiting for you to get back."

He smiled, resolved, and reached up to kiss her.

"I'll be right back, I swear."

She nodded, pushing him from the room.

Luke stopped in the doorway, looking over his shoulder at her for a second, before running down the hall and out of the house.

In his absence, her limbs grew cold again. The sun went into hiding. The fire blew out.

Kira dropped to her knees, clutching her chest.

It was finally time.

Chapter Sixteen

She promised.

Kira had made a promise, and she didn't intend on breaking it. Not this time.

When Luke got back, Kira would be there waiting. Not the Kira who was a step away from madness. Not the deranged Kira who lusted for blood.

No.

A Protector Kira. A sane Kira.

Luke's Kira.

So as she dropped fully to the floor, Kira held her powers close to her heart and let the shadows come. It was time to end it. She couldn't fight the darkness any longer.

Her body jerked. Seizures racked her limbs.

But Kira was beyond everything.

She was swimming through fire, riding her flames as they circled her body, holding them tightly under her skin.

Kira was searching for the source, the switch, the part of her that decided Punisher or Protector, because she was ready to say goodbye to the anger, to the kill.

So she kept pushing, deeper and deeper into her soul. That was the story of the two angels after all. Whether they were real or myth, they were Kira. She was two people, two powers, two lives.

Well, she had chosen a path, but actually letting her Punisher's powers go? That was a different issue. That was the only factor left, the one thing holding her back. Because she had thought it would be easy, that she would decide, and naturally the other half of her would fade away.

But her decision had been set the moment Luke walked through the door, and her Punisher powers still burned inside her heart.

And the deeper she sank, the stronger everything seemed to become. Her Protector fire and Punisher flames melded together, red and yellow, dancing across her mind until everything around her was orange, and there was no differentiating the two.

Kira pulled at the fire, willed it apart, but it wouldn't go. It wouldn't tear.

Kira delved further, until her skin was so hot it was as though she walked on the surface of the sun itself, in a place where there were no Protectors, no Punishers, no angels, just a light so bright it would blind anyone who dared open their eyes to look.

"God?" she called, forgetting that she was speaking into her own mind. It didn't feel that way. It felt divine. Sacred.

No response.

"Will you save me? Like you saved the originals?" she asked meekly. The words scratched her dry throat, ripping their way out of her body.

But no one was listening. No one was there.

Kira was alone. More alone than she had ever felt before.

Lost even.

So she ran, racing back the way she came, following the fire out of her heart, riding the waves until she was in her own skin. But it wasn't her own. A foreign host had taken over, black and writhing, sticking to every part of her.

Teeth dug deep into her lip.

Kira willed them away.

But they wouldn't budge.

She was turning into a vampire. For good this time.

Her body had rejected her, had kicked her out. Somehow, Kira had been pushed over the edge.

She screamed, a loud, frustrated cry.

It hadn't worked. She had been sure it would work. That choosing would be key. That her powers would obey.

But Kira had been betrayed by her own fire. Abandoned by it. Even now, her fingers felt colder. Her toes were like ice.

A small smolder still lit her heart, but it was flickering, fading.

How long before it was gone?

Before she was gone?

No, Kira opened her eyes. The world was sharper around her, clearer, as though she could see even the molecules of air hanging invisible around her. She had seen like this once before, in a dream, in a life she never wanted.

Kira stood, lightning fast.

She had to get to the wall. It didn't matter that there were vampires, that Aldrich was waiting for her, ready to strike.

She was in transition, and the UV radiation of the wall was the only thing that could save her.

Kira reached out with her mind, searching for Luke, wishing he could somehow hear her. But there was no wall, no connection to his mind. There was only emptiness.

So instead she whispered, "I'm sorry," knowing no one was close enough to hear. But somehow, the words would find him. He would find a way to understand why she had broken her promise. He would find a way to forgive her.

But before she could run, a scent tickled her nose. Sweet. Innocent.

Childlike.

Kira covered her mouth, holding back the urge with sheer will. Her entire body stilled, glued to the spot while her still conscious mind waged war against the shadows clouding her judgment. She refused to turn into an animal.

A steady beat thrummed in her ears, a delicate thud, a pitter-patter of small feet, or was it the pump of a small heart?

The noise. The smell. They grew, louder, stronger, harder to ignore, until Kira's entire brain was taken over by the two senses.

But her feet held still, immobile, somehow still under her command.

"Kira?"

She sucked in a breath. She recognized that high-pitched voice, still not hit by puberty.

"Kira?"

Should couldn't turn, couldn't look at him. She would break.

"Get out of here," Kira croaked. Her voice was harsh, unrecognizable.

"It's me. TJ. Luke told me to come after the meeting, he told me to go with all the other kids. I tried to tell him I'm not a kid, that I can fight, but he wouldn't listen. But I couldn't leave, not without Patrick's teddy bear. He's my best friend, Patrick, and I know how scared he gets, I know he needs his teddy..."

Kira tuned him out. She couldn't listen to anymore. Couldn't bear the strength in his little voice. It called to her. It would taste so good, such earnestness, it would sing.

But it was Luke's brother, the part of her that was still there yelled, Luke's little brother.

Her palms twitched. Her fingers stretched, getting ready to strike.

But as she whipped around, ready to grab him by the throat, another person Kira was afraid had died awakened inside of her.

"Get out," she bellowed, screamed at TJ, instantly falling back down, crawling away from the look of confusion and fear written all over that little boy's face.

And before she knew what she was doing, Kira jumped. She pushed off of her feet, springing through the window behind her, not caring as glass cut deeply into her skin.

Instincts took over. She landed cat-like on her feet and took off at a sprint, running for the wall.

The conduits were there. Their blood swam into her senses, pushing her forward.

But another girl pushed her forward too, a conduit girl struggling to get free, pushing her toward a wall of fire that would burn her alive or save her.

Kira didn't know which.

She just knew she had to keep running.

And she did. She flew—her feet moving faster than ever before, pounding against the pavement. Trees swished by her, blurred and barely there except for the variations of green in the peripheral of her eyes.

She saw no one. No conduit teams, no vampires. Was the battle still raging? Had someone won? Was she the only wild card left?

And then she was on the main road, charging farther and farther out of Sonnyville, closer and closer to—

Blood.

A giant pool of blood.

It drifted into her senses, pulling her forward, enticing her. Kira could sense it at the wall—conduit blood, Protector blood.

And without a doubt, she knew one taste was all it would take. One taste and she would be gone forever. But the vampire in charge of her body didn't care, had no thought except for the blood, had no goal except to drink it.

Kira was trapped. She fought against it, but her efforts were futile. She had lost control. Her only hope was that the blood lay outside the wall, beyond Sonnyville.

As she approached, her laser vision took over, zooming in on the blood, locating it.

Just beyond the wall, there was a car resting undamaged in the middle of the road. Burnt tires mixed with the sweetness of the blood, filling Kira's senses. And the blood was there, pooling next to the driver's seat, dripping free from two holes in a blond man's neck. He was leaning upside down, draped out of the car and onto the pavement, dropped there by a vampire who wanted to leave Kira a message.

The conduit inside of her screamed, cried out, prayed *please no.*

The vampire controlling her kept running—vision slipping in closer, focused on two puncture wounds. Her teeth ached to fill the void.

And then the wall was there.

Kira slammed into it, lifting off of her feet, flipping over onto her back with the force of the blow. The sun dug into her. UV burned her skin until it started to flake, to crack with the heat.

Her voice cried out, whimpering in pain.

Her soul sang, triumphant.

The flames awakened inside of her heart, called out by the wall, almost like a familiar friend. The conduit inside of her started pushing, fighting the vampire away.

The blackness started budging, more resistant than usual, leaving a permanent residue inside of her limbs. Kira couldn't clear it all away. The shadows were lurking, and her fire, even with the wall, wasn't strong enough to remove them entirely. But it was enough for the moment.

Kira was in control again.

The teeth biting into her lip shrunk, slightly at first, until they were dulled down, only somewhat sharper than normal. The strength in her arms ebbed, and she dropped completely limp to the ground. Her skin, crackled from the fire, now called for the sun and began to seal closed, smooth and tanned once more.

But it was only temporary, and Kira's heart sank with the truth of that statement. Her own fire wasn't enough anymore. Her fire, which had been strong enough to kill any vampire that crossed her path, to break through their immunity even, wasn't strong enough to crush the one vampire she needed to end—the one inside of her.

Without the wall, she would fall. And there was no magic cure, no way to save herself. There was only death. Maybe that had been her only option all along—she was just too stubborn to see it.

And then Kira remembered—the boy, the car, the blood.

She stood, slowly, achingly, fighting against sore limbs. But she preferred it to the zip, to the lightning speed, because this was human—almost.

Blinking, Kira tried to bring back her vision, and it came slowly, but the world looked fuzzy. The clarity was missing. The perfect sight was gone. But she could see enough.

"Luke?" Kira cried, her mind running on overdrive. The boy in the car was dead, but was he Luke? The blond hair could look familiar. His back was to her, but his long build could be Luke's. His neck looked a little too stocky, his fingers a little too fat, his stomach a little too soft.

And then Kira took note of the collar around his neck, the buttons running down the center of his shirt, and she breathed, sighing in relief.

No way was that Luke. And when she said that to herself, she could finally see this man, see all the ways he definitely was not her Luke.

But he was someone's friend, someone's husband, someone's father even. And now he was dead. And it was all Kira's fault.

The battle, the one she was hiding from, the one she couldn't fight, it was all about her. It was about her saving Tristan, about her potential to fall, about her fight with Aldrich.

And staring death in the face, she yelled in frustration, because she was even more trapped now than ever before. Four feet forward, three feet back, fifteen to the left and five to the right. The wall. Her box. Her prison.

"Aldrich!" Kira cried out.

No answer.

"Aldrich!" she yelled again, ripping her vocal chords with the force of her scream. She wanted him there, wanted him to watch her die, wanted him to know that in the end Kira was strong enough to do the only thing she could—to keep the shadows at bay, to keep herself from falling, and to keep the conduits safe from her destruction.

But before she did, Kira closed her eyes, holding back the tears threatening to spill from her eyes. Before she let death take over, she wanted to say goodbye. Her mother and father would still have Chloe. Tristan hardly remembered her, and Pavia would keep him safe.

But Luke, he would be alone. And she chose him, she wanted to be with him, but fate had never been on her side.

So Kira opened her mind, feeling for the path inside his head. She didn't want to be alone when she died. She wanted to be with him, safe and sound in the comfort of his love.

But he wasn't there.

Confused, Kira searched for his thoughts, for their connection. Had the darkness broken them? Broken their bond like it had broken everything else inside of her?

But no, the path to his mind was open, but where was Luke? He was blank. There was no love, no strength, no resolve bubbling down her limbs, bringing her joy like it normally did. There was just eerie silence.

Her heart began to pound as a sinking fear settled in.

What had happened to Luke?

Eyes shooting open, Kira scanned the ground around her, but there was no sign of him. She walked around the perimeter of the wall, as far out of the UV radiation she dared move, but he wasn't there.

She couldn't leave without saying goodbye. He was her strength, her rock—she couldn't do this without him.

Reaching into her pocket, Kira dialed his number.

Ring.

Ring.

Ring.

Click.

No voicemail. No message. Not even the sound of his voice to make her feel better.

Kira tried again, but it was more of the same.

She clicked on the keypad, texting him, but she had very little hope of any response. She looked up again.

The car. The conduit.

It was odd. The two of them there, on the other side of the wall. Strange. Why would any conduit have driven through the wall, willingly bringing himself into vampire territory?

The answer was simple. He wouldn't.

But something else could—someone else could.

And Kira remembered the smell of burnt tires. She looked closer at the ground, where black streaks stamped the concrete.

This car wasn't driven over the other side of the wall. It was forced there, kicking and screaming. And there was only one person in the world who could do that.

Aldrich.

Aldrich with his telekinesis.

Kira's head snapped up, alert. He was out there somewhere, she was sure of it. He was watching her, silently laughing at her struggle, gleeful with the knowledge that she was at the point of no return.

And Luke had to be with him—unconscious, but not dead, because she could still feel him on the other side of the bond, still knew he was breathing, but his mind was still.

Just like a movie was playing in her head, Kira could see what had happened. Luke had run from her grandparent's house, searched the town square and his own home for TJ. But TJ had been at Patrick's house, had been getting his best friend his teddy, and Luke would have never thought to look there.

No, he thought his brother wanted to join the fight with the grown-ups. So Luke found a Protector with a car and hopped inside, driving aimlessly through the town looking for TJ to no avail. And then the two of them decided to search closer to the wall. And as soon as they hit the main road, Aldrich sensed them, and took control, using his mind to drag the car across the barrier.

He knew exactly who it was, exactly what he was doing. And somehow, he knew that Kira had chosen Luke, that Luke would be the key.

Kira envisioned it. Luke must have known. They probably tried the car door, but the stubborn locks remained shut, held by Aldrich's mental control. The glass wouldn't break. The windows wouldn't roll down. They had been trapped, knowing that death was near.

As soon as they crossed the wall, Aldrich struck, killing the Protector and knocking Luke unconscious, waiting for Kira to come. Probably arranging the car and the conduit's body just for her. And Kira had played right into his plan, but she had no other choice.

And now Luke needed her.

"Aldrich," she said softly, calmly, "I know you're there. Come out so we can end this."

There was no answer. He wanted her to beg.

Kira knelt down, seemingly tying her shoe, and pulled out the pocketknife. She would need this soon. Hiding it in her palm, she stood again, tucking the knife into her back pocket.

Time to start the show.

"What do you want?" she called into the trees. "I'll do anything to save him!" The crack in her voice was real. The shake in her hands was real too.

"Please, just let me see him," Kira whimpered.

But there was still no response.

"Aldrich," she cried, letting the tears fall down her cheeks. Her body mirrored their movement as she slipped to her knees, a beggar.

"I'll do anything," she said one last time.

And then she heard it. Leaves rustling, branches breaking, footsteps.

A body flew from the trees, landing roughly on the asphalt with a smack. And this time, it was Luke—limp, immobile. Dead almost, but the bond in her head gave Kira hope that somehow he was still alive.

She started to run for him, but stopped herself. She was in a cage, trapped inside the fire. But he needed her, Kira struggled, she had to do something.

And then a voice sounded.

"It's simple," Aldrich said, still hiding in the forest, "I want you to try to save him."

Kira searched for the vampire, but Aldrich was nowhere in sight. And she refused to fight a ghost.

"Show yourself," she demanded. Her hands had balled into iron fists and the sun had already started strengthening, gathering in her core. The shadows were there too, just waiting to strike.

And then more leaves, more branches breaking.

Kira followed the sound.

Aldrich stepped free of the woods and Kira stepped back in horror.

Chapter Seventeen

This was not the Aldrich Kira remembered.

Not the tall, elegantly dressed, arrogant jerk. Gone was his slicked back light-brown hair, his calm and cruel demeanor. The only parts of him she recognized were the cold, almost black, midnight blue eyes.

The man before her was a monster.

And Kira had made him that way.

His skin was burnt, charred black and crusted over. His hair was singed off, replaced by blood-red scalded flesh. His nose had melted away, turned into a stub, and his ears looked completely gone.

His body hunched over, unable to stand straight because his back was so terribly injured. He moved with a limp, his vampire strength seemingly tapped out. And his clothes were baggy, ill fitting, hiding what Kira knew was a broken body.

Her hand came up and clamped over her mouth, catching the gasp she had let escape.

Unable to look anywhere else, Kira caught his eyes, the one part of him that remained unharmed. And they looked at her, calculating and full of hatred.

"What's wrong, Kira? You don't want to look at your masterpiece?" he asked coolly, shuffling closer to Luke.

She shivered. "I never meant for that to happen." And she didn't.

"No, you just meant to kill me and be done with it," he said, smiling.

"No worse than your plans for me." Kira returned his overly sweet grin, pushing any feelings of sympathy for Aldrich to the side. He was a monster, and now his body just reflected what was in his heart.

"No matter." Aldrich shrugged. "A decade from now I will be fully healed and back to my former self. I don't think you'll be as lucky."

He knelt down, and brushed the hair off of Luke's face.

Kira's body jerked forward in protest. "Don't touch him."

Aldrich's head snapped in her direction, and his eyes flashed an icy blue. "Make me."

Kira stepped forward, closing in on the edge of the wall, but then she stopped. She couldn't go any farther without losing herself, without falling. She was trapped.

Frustrated, Kira lifted her hands, flinging Punisher flames at Aldrich. She could kill him from here. She didn't need to move.

But a tree branch smacked her forearms, throwing her palms to the side and her flames exploded aimlessly into the trees opposite Aldrich, useless.

He cackled, sending a shiver of pure anger down her spine. One way or another Kira would end him. Her fingers crunched into a fist.

"This is too much," he said, glee evident in his voice. "Our dear Kira trapped in the very fire she yearns to hold onto, unable to fight for her love." He slid a nail down Luke's cheek, staring Kira straight in the eye as he rubbed a stubby finger over the cut and brought it to his mouth, tasting the blood that leaked from the fresh wound.

Kira bit her lip, trying not to lose control. The power inside of her surged, begging for release. But it was clear that Aldrich was goading her. He wouldn't kill Luke, not yet, not before he was done playing games.

Aldrich stood quickly and walked around Luke's body, closer to the wall. "I wonder what will make you break?" he asked, reaching out as if to touch her cheek. His hand stopped just shy of the invisible line, not crossing into the UV radiation currently burning into Kira's skin, filling her with hope and strength. She might be trapped, but it was a cage that Aldrich couldn't break into.

She remained silent, not giving in to his taunt.

"You know," he said, drawing his hand back. His eyes lost focus as his brain sifted back, bringing up a memory. "I knew what was happening the moment you let me go. I saw the fight in your eyes, the battle raging inside your veins, I could feel the shadows flood your heart. I knew in that moment, that no matter what happened, I had won. Because there is no going back, Kira. Once you've tasted the darkness, there is no stopping it."

"But there is," she said quietly, not really believing it herself.

"What? Are you talking about Tristan? Yes, yes, I've heard all about how you saved him," he drawled. "I'm afraid it's all anyone can talk about. I'm rather sick of it, to be honest."

"Because you lost that battle," Kira said, smug, letting a grin curl her lips.

Aldrich's eyes flashed, his crackled flesh tensed up. "What battle? Tristan is a fool who fell in love with a girl who could never love him back."

Kira's hand shook. Fire pressed against her palms, aching to be let out, but she held it steady, letting her powers bubble up and strengthen, waiting for the right time. "That's not true."

"It's not? Then where is he? Why is Luke our special guest and not Tristan?"

"I loved him enough to let him go, something you'll never understand."

"Such sentimental drivel," Aldrich said, chuckling to himself. "You still don't understand, Kira. I tried to tell you before, but you just don't understand."

"By all means, enlighten me." Kira crossed her arms, trying to keep the conversation going as long as possible. In the back of her mind, Kira was just waiting for the right moment to strike. Because he would falter, he would lose control, and the moment he did, Kira would attack. She had to. There was no other way for this to end. There never was.

"You're a realist, Kira." He sighed and Kira rolled her eyes. *Not this again*, she thought.

"So what?"

"Realists can't choose love, they don't know how. Love is for the believers, love is the ultimate faith—that invisible idea people will build their lives on. But a realist just doesn't understand that—they need the facts, the logic—they can't take the leap. They don't know how to put love first."

"While I'm really enjoying the psychobabble, can you just get to the point?" Kira asked.

"The point is that I know you will fight me because if you don't, I will kill this boy." He stepped closer, his voice deepening. "The point is that I know you will fall because as much as you say you are in love, you don't really know how to believe in love." He looked at her, his eyes turning black, his burnt face glowing in triumph. "The point is, I will win and you will lose, as much as you tell yourself differently."

Kira leapt forward, rage pushing her movements. Fire flew from her hands, surging toward Aldrich in a wave of crushing heat. He was wrong. Kira had loved Tristan and she loved Luke now, and no one would use fancy words to try to take that away. She wasn't some unfeeling robot. She wasn't. And Kira would show Aldrich just how wrong he was.

But as soon as Kira crossed the line, her fire wavered, losing its heat and the darkness crept forward, breaking through her skin, pushing the teeth back out, spreading a numbing cold throughout her body.

Her anger rolled away, replaced by a deep hunger she had yet to give into. Luke's blood surged into her thoughts.

She wanted it.

She wanted one taste. Just one.

No!

Kira threw herself backward, back into her prison, and fire surged through her body. She panted and let the flames take over, let them chase the shadows away, another temporary fix, but a fix nonetheless.

The blood pounding in her ears began to slow.

A high-pitched squeal replaced it, flooding her senses, and clapping hands brought a surge of hatred back into her heart.

Slowly, Kira stood and turned around, meeting Aldrich's smirk with a glare. That didn't prove anything, no matter what he said.

But he didn't try to speak—his eyes did the talking for him. Hot white with barely a hint of blue, they were practically alight with his excitement. Aldrich thought he was winning.

And in the back of her mind, Kira agreed.

To her right, the passenger side door of the car broke off, screeching loudly. Kira couldn't help but stare as it scraped along the ground in her direction, lifting up over her head to land behind her, just inside of the wall.

Her gaze raced back to Aldrich, to his wide, victorious eyes.

The metal behind her crunched, bending in on itself, making a semicircular cocoon.

Kira's heart began to race. There was nowhere she could run. She was trapped.

The scuffle of metal on concrete sent fear into her heart—it was getting louder, closer, until a coolness stung her arm.

She was being pushed forward. The door had her trapped, and all Kira could stare at was the almost invisible line of the wall, the slight quiver of heat that showed where the blast of UV ended.

The spot expanded, growing larger until it took up her entire line of vision.

Kira tried to reach for her back pocket, for the knife she had kept hidden, but the metal was too close, was closing in on her, trapping her.

And then the hunger lurched in her stomach, a craving for the conduit blood resting just a few feet away, waiting for her.

Digging her feet in the ground, Kira tried to resist. But she couldn't fight it—none of it.

Luke's finger twitched. He was waking up.

Waking up just in time to feel Kira's bite.

But then the door dropped to the ground, clanging loudly, stopping Kira millimeters from the edge of the wall.

"It would be so easy," Aldrich said slowly, "but I want to see you break yourself."

Luke moaned and rolled to the side. His eyes remained shut. His body stilled. It was almost as if he was reminding Kira that he was still there, still alive, still worth fighting for.

She stepped back into the fire, her mind running on overdrive.

It was time.

She whimpered.

Kira wasn't ready to say goodbye.

Not to life and not to Luke.

But Aldrich was right. She was a realist. She would fall. She couldn't make that leap. She had tried giving up her Punisher powers and it had failed, because some part of her really didn't believe that happiness was in her future, really didn't believe that love would cure everything, really didn't believe that her life could be one dream come true.

The moment she was born, she had been doomed. Her life wasn't a fairytale. It was a nightmare. She was a force of destruction, a killing machine, death to any vampire who dared cross her path.

And the last thing she would do on this earth was destroy this man who had taken so much away from her.

Aldrich stepped back, kneeling over Luke's body, keeping eye contact with Kira the entire time. He lifted Luke, holding his slackened body upright. Luke groaned in protest. His eyes started to flutter.

Aldrich tilted Luke's head to the side, exposing his neck. Fangs extended, pushing through his closed lips, and a sinister grin widened his mouth.

He was goading her, urging Kira to make her move, to fall.

Kira brought her hands behind her back and reached into her pocket, flicking the knife open and letting the cool metal touch the fragile skin at her wrist.

She was going to die.

But she was taking Aldrich with her.

Breathing deeply, Kira bit her lip, trying to keep the pain from her face as the razor blade cut deep into her skin, searing flesh and veins. Blood dripped down her fingers, slipping to the ground below, and the shadows followed it. The moment she chose death, made the ultimate sacrifice, the vampire inside of her vanished, leaving only fire in its place.

Aldrich raised his brows, confused, pausing for a moment as the smell of her untainted blood drifted into his senses. He hesitated, dropping Luke an inch.

And Kira attacked.

Flames soared from her palms, blasting into Aldrich so hard that his feet lifted and he flew backward, smacking the ground with his burnt and bald skull. Surprise was etched into his features.

But Kira couldn't stop. Already her life was fading. Her fire flickered. Her body was running on adrenaline, so she pounced, jumping free of the wall to land on Aldrich's chest.

Her fire sunk into his skin, burning already charred flesh. And he was weak. Her powers had sapped his strength. His eyes were glazed over, unfocused from the heavy fall he had just taken.

Kira pressed on, wrapping her hands around his neck, focusing all of her strength on that single spot. Her fingers burned, the lava pouring through her veins was starting to hurt, but she didn't pay attention to that. Her eyes scanned Aldrich's face, at the cracks spreading along his features, at the life leaving his black eyes.

It was almost over.

A branch flew from the trees, bumping into her arm, but it was barely a nudge, barely strong enough for Kira to feel let alone be hurt by.

Another hit her back.

Kira remained where she was.

The blood from her wrist poured over Aldrich's melting skin, dying it red, mixing with the charcoal flaking off of his neck.

Her fire was starting to slow. But not from the shadows—not from the darkness, which had disappeared. Her life was leaking away and her power was going with it.

Kira's vision started to spot.

She blinked. *Not yet*, she urged, *hold on just a little longer.*

Pushing one last time, her power surged. The unstoppable mix of Punisher and Protector sunk into Aldrich.

And it worked.

Her fire severed his neck, melting his flesh away, burning bone so severely that it cracked in half. His eyes widened, realizing his death was inevitable. He was frozen in place as the shadow crept up his neck, a wave of darkness that wasn't vampirism, but was ash—the smoke of his skin flaking away into nothing.

Kira dropped a few inches, landing on the ground with a thud.

Aldrich was gone.

He was finally gone.

Kira had won. *But at what price?* she wondered, rolling to the side. The blackness had left her body, and for the first time in ages, her fire felt pure, untainted. Her skin felt exactly like her own.

But even that awareness was fading.

"Kira?" Luke's voice filled her ears. Her heart lifted. She would get to say goodbye.

Shuffling feet. Clothes scraping asphalt. And then a hand touched her cheek, a warm hand, hot against her cooling skin.

She was lifted, moved so her head rested on his lap. Kira looked into his fiery eyes, at the emerald green around the edges, adoring how they glowed with love.

"You did it," he said, his voice filled with awe. "You killed Aldrich. We won."

He wiped his thumb along her cheek, brushing away the tears. Confusion clouded over as she remained silent. He scanned her face, looking for injuries, moving down her body, searching for the problem, and then he froze, eyes widening in horror.

"Kira, what did you do?" He cursed, begging for an explanation.

Using the last bits of her strength, Kira raised her palm to his cheek, catching the tears that were falling. He had to understand.

"I saved you," she said, her voice barely a whisper, "I saved you all from me."

"We found a cure, there was another way." He shook his head. His lips wavered and the body below her head trembled.

"No." Kira sighed. "There wasn't. But Luke?"

He nodded.

"I wish there had been. Because I do love you."

"I love you too," he told her, voice cracking. And then he leaned down, planting a soft kiss upon her lips.

Her vision began to fade. The world around her seemed to evaporate until all she saw was Luke. His features hardened, the word "no" danced across his lips.

She felt him lift her, felt the pull of gravity as she sagged in his arms. He carried her, placing her gently down, running to the side.

Kira felt the rumble of the car.

He was speaking to her. She couldn't hear the words he was saying, but it was okay. She kept looking at him, drinking him in until her heavy lids fell shut.

But it wasn't dark or empty or void behind her closed eyes, because with death so close, there was nothing for Kira but her dreams. The world had disappeared. There were no smells, no sounds, no sights to take in except those her mind created.

So she dreamed of the life she could have had. The one she wanted to have if things had been different.

Instead of finding her on the ground, lying there like a fading memory, Luke would have turned to see Kira standing over him, waiting for him. He would have stood and she would have leapt into his arms, overjoyed at their victory. He would have spun her around, laughing together so blissfully that nothing could outshine them.

And they would have lived together, happily ever after—joking together, bickering with each other, kissing fights away, making memories—they would tease each other mercilessly but would always know that at the base of it there was love. And not the kind of love built on lust, not the kind that eventually puttered out. But real love, the kind of love built on something stronger, built on knowing that you could bare your soul to another person and he would do the same. The sort of love that brightened the world around you, making everything better because you knew your best friend would also be your forever.

Kira let the dream fill her as she traveled back to the place she had been only an hour before, into the heart of her fire, into her core.

The world around her was in flames, but it wasn't scary. It was her power keeping her safe, keeping her warm, reassuring her that even though her life was over, it wasn't the end of everything.

But most of all, it wasn't scary because Luke was there, arm draped over her shoulder, pulling her in close, telling Kira she would never be alone, that they would be together forever. Kira listened to his words. She let the devotion in his voice roll over her. She let herself believe in him, in them, in herself.

They kissed and her mind was filled with love. It tingled down her senses—a warm golden glow that made life and even death taste sweeter.

And without her realizing it, her soul split. The Punisher fire drifted away, evaporating into the heat of their love.

For the first time in her short life, Kira was at peace, wrapped soothingly in her dreams.

But after a while, even the dreams faded away.

Epilogue

Lana Peters stepped out of the car as quickly as her old body would allow. Two Protector councilmen followed, quiet and stoic, more like bodyguards than a greeting crew. So Lana smiled for the lot of them, forcing her cheeks to widen even though her wrinkled hands shook.

It was hard to let old fears go, too hard for most of the town. But Lana knew, from her daughter and from her granddaughter, that some rules needed to be broken and some traditions needed to fade into the past.

Which was why she had volunteered to welcome the dozen or so vampires standing in a straight line just beyond the wall. Without them, the battle would have lasted far longer. Without them, many more conduit lives would have likely been lost. Without them, her own husband, who believed himself to be twenty years younger than he really was, might have fallen.

She smiled softly to herself, picturing him. He did not want her in this role, but what else could the wife of the head councilman do? The grandmother of the very girl who promised these vampires their lives back? It was her duty, the least she could do. Kira would have wanted nothing else.

"Welcome," Lana called, strengthening her voice from its normal dainty singsong. "We have turned the wall off. You are free to come in, as friends."

All of the vampires looked at each other, quick sidelong glances that were hard for Lana to follow with her old, human eyes. But she did notice the bright blue hue to their irises—a color that matched the sunny, cloudless sky.

And then one broke free from the line, approaching the wall guardedly. She was a girl with long, flowing black hair who looked no older than twenty to Lana. Too young to be so mature. And right behind her was a boy that Lana did recognize—Tristan. A visitor in their town only a few days before, who looked rather nervous himself.

"Hello, Lana Peters," the vampire spoke, "I'm Pavia. I think Kira." She paused, swallowed. "I mean Luke probably mentioned me."

"Yes, of course, I've heard about you. So nice to finally meet you in person." She nodded slightly, an old-fashioned woman-to-woman handshake.

Pavia shrugged and grinned. "So, should we get this party started? One-way road to mortality and all that jazz?"

Lana coughed, hiding a laugh for the benefit of the

stodgy councilmen at her side. "Yes, of course. Please take a seat in the car behind this one and we will take you to the town square."

"Perfect." She turned around, speaking to her own people. "All right everyone, you heard the woman. Keep those fangs securely locked away." She turned again, grabbing Tristan's hand and tugging him along, speaking into his ear. The boy visibly relaxed and walked with Pavia ahead of the other vampires.

Lana eased back into her car with a little help from the two conduits next to her. And then the cars started moving, making their way back into the only home Lana had ever known. She was born in Sonnyville, met her husband here, raised her child here. Her house held the stories of her life. The shelf her husband had accidentally hung crooked, the old chair her father had made for them as a wedding gift, the spot where her daughter had taken her first little baby steps, the spot where she had taken her last.

Never in that life were vampires in her little town. It was a safe haven, an oasis from the threat of vampires, and having them here did feel somehow wrong. But also right at the same time. Because more than anything, her life was about trying to protect people—from vampires, from hardships, from heartache. And now Protectors would be able to protect lost souls in the way they were originally created to do—her granddaughter Kira had been right about that.

But not everyone agreed, Lana thought, looking around at the homes they were driving past. Half were empty, their patrons gathered at the town square to celebrate what had been a victorious battle and now a victorious new future for conduits to step into. But half were full of curious eyes staring out the window and of children locked tightly in their rooms. Half were resistant and doubtful, stuck in their ways.

Lana reached her heavy arm out, pressing the window down, still marveling that the push of a button was all it took—quick and easy. In a world of so much technology, it seemed only right for her people to finally start advancing too.

She waved hello to all of the families still huddled inside their homes, trying to let them know that there was nothing to fear.

Before long, a sea of blond heads came into view, her people—a good portion of them—gathered in the town square, waiting for their guests.

The driver pulled over and opened her door, giving Lana a helping hand as she stepped free of the car. She motioned for him to open the door of the other car as well. Pavia stepped out first, to the gasp of the entire village, but she seemed unaffected and strode toward Lana.

Such gusto, Lana smiled, this vampire almost reminded her of Kira, the confidence and strength.

Her smile wavered, cracked. She took a deep breath

and began shuffling her tired feet toward the dais, toward the comforting presence of her husband. Based on the stares of the conduits she ambled past, the vampires were following.

Just short of the steps, Lana stopped, signaling her guests to continue. The council platform was not her place. Her place was the empty chair a few steps away, the one she had been sitting in for half of her life while she watched her husband work. So she sat, and tuned out the speech she had all but memorized the evening before. Instead, she let the baritone voice she loved relax her as she looked around at her people.

Some were afraid. Some were hopeful. Some wary. Some excited.

Her gaze moved farther up, toward the seven men in their fanciest suits sitting mightily on their thrones—a sign of strength for the new, potentially rough road ahead. In the middle, her husband, fanned by some of their closest friends. But those weren't the faces Lana was searching for.

To the left of her council, still sitting but on smaller chairs, were eight redhaired men. Seven made up the Punisher Council and the last was Noah, the man who had come to testify against Kira, who had argued to end her life. His face was composed, hard to read, but she wondered what he was thinking now.

Lana's gaze shifted to the right, and her heart slipped a little, sagged even more than the normally heavy heart of someone who had lived so long, endured too much. Luke was standing beside the thrones, alone, hands clenched behind his back. His face was impassive, too melancholic for such a young, healthy, vibrant man. His eyes were red, puffy from long days spent in a similar fashion to Lana's—crying.

Blinking away new tears, Lana focused on her husband again. His speech was coming to a close.

"…this great new day. And so, we venture forward together—once enemies and now allies, trying to find the solution my granddaughter sought to provide. Pavia," he said, gesturing to the vampire, and she stepped forward, "has been brave enough to volunteer, to entrust her life to Luke and Noah as they try to restore her humanity according to the method Kira described before." He paused, his shoulders hunched an inch. "Before the hard won battle a few days ago."

Lana, like the rest of the town, turned her attention to Pavia. Her skin was pale, pearly in the sunlight, and her eyes glowed a stark blue that jumped from her face. Her smile was easy, but Lana saw the catch in her throat, the tense rigidity in her body. And it humanized the vampire. She was nervous, as anyone would be to experiment with his or her life, even a life that had been lived far longer than nature intended.

Pavia continued to step forward. The town remained so quiet that even Lana's old ears heard the click of shoes on wood. The vampire paused, and then let her body sink into the lounge chair waiting in the center of the platform.

Luke walked forward first, leaning down to say something to the girl, something that made her stiff body relax. She moved fast, so that her hand was just a blur, but Lana knew what occurred. The vampire had reached out to squeeze Luke's hand, to return the comforting favor.

Noah joined the two, completing the trio, and the entire town breathed in.

Flames erupted on Luke's palms.

His hand shifted forward, closing in on the vampire's skin.

Pavia flinched.

"Stop!"

And everyone obeyed.

Like statues, no one moved. And then, shocked, the sea of blond shifted together, focusing all of their attentions on the source of that command.

Lana's breath caught.

Standing there at the top of the square was the exact replica of her daughter, of her baby girl Lana, almost at the same age as the last time she had seen her. Stick-straight blond hair, tanned skin, green flaming eyes, tall and proud stance. But it wasn't Lana. It was not a ghost come back to haunt, it was Kira. A one hundred percent Protector Kira.

A grin spread across Lana's face, shifting wrinkles, bringing youth back to her features.

Kira was alive. Her granddaughter was alive.

"Really? You guys started without me? One little coma," Kira paused, cocking her hip to the side. "Well, I guess that was technically my second coma, but come on, it's only been a few days. Way quicker than last time."

Still the image of her mother to Lana, Kira strode forward, all attitude. "You're acting like I'm dead. No faith." She shook her head, and then stopped, a smile breaking through the chiding façade.

And Lana knew why as feet thudded loudly down the steps behind her and a body flew into her vision.

Before Kira could say another word, Luke was there, lifting her up, spinning her around, kissing her. Their reunion was full of so much joy, so much happiness that it brightened the world around them, cascaded around the square like a surge of power. Laughter rained down on the crowd, infectious, bringing smiles to the faces of every conduit there.

Lana looked away, letting the couple share a few moments without scrutiny. Her eyes searched for those of her husband, and found them alight, proud. His eyes shifted, met Lana's, and in that second, it was like their entire lives flashed between them, and they knew that somehow, it was all meant to be. Everything their family had endured, it was all meant to be.

Hands clutched fiercely together, Kira and Luke walked back into view, moving as one toward the platform.

Pavia was out of her chair, waiting for them, arms crossed.

"Cutting it a little close, don't you think?"

"What, you didn't trust me?" Luke teased and Pavia just raised her eyebrow.

"With good reason," Kira drawled, elbowing him playfully in the ribs. He just hugged her close, kissing the top of her head. Kira protested, but Lana knew her granddaughter, and there was no real fight in her body as she leaned into that kiss.

Behind them, her husband coughed, urging the children to move a little quicker, and Lana laughed quietly to herself—so much personality for one little wooden stage to contain.

Pavia returned to her seat, sitting a little taller this time, with a little more confidence. Luke moved to stand next to Noah.

Kira shifted her gaze and Lana followed it to Tristan. He was watching her politely and inclined his head in hello. Kira lifted one corner of her lip, sad but happy at the same time, and greeted him the same way. Then Tristan's eyes shifted, returning to Pavia, and Kira nodded to herself, satisfied, before walking over next to Luke.

"Ready?" she asked Pavia. The vampire nodded.

Luke brought a flame to his palm, the fire caught Lana's eyes, but Kira pushed his hand to the side. His brows furrowed.

"I can do this," Kira said, just loud enough for Lana to hear, but the words filled her with a sense of peace. Her granddaughter was an incredibly strong woman.

And even at only eighteen, Kira lifted her arm, the wrist wrapped in a bandage, as a sign of her resolve. Almost instantly, flames erupted above her hand, sizzling and crackling as though alive. Her powers were still strong, but now they were pure Protector. Even from her seat on the sideline, Lana felt the difference.

And the fire grew, expanding to encase the vampire's entire body, burning into cool flesh. Pavia didn't flinch. That was how confident she was.

Kira nodded to Noah.

He brought a Punisher flame to his palm—it was darker, different, and completely foreign to Lana. But not to Kira. Together they worked—two powers and two people.

At first, Pavia's flesh began to burn, but after a while, the crusted skin flaked off to reveal smooth, pink, human flesh.

But Lana had stopped watching the vampire and had shifted her attention to her granddaughter instead. A grin spread from ear to ear, brighter than the flames shooting from Kira's palms. Her eyes sparkled as they looked out at the crowd, at Tristan, and finally at Luke.

And one thought entered Lana's mind—she wished her daughter was there to see it, was alive to see what she had created, because Kira was perfect.

She had saved the world.

She had saved her people.

But most of all, she had proved exactly what Lana's daughter had been begging her mother to understand all along—that love would prevail.

Love of a world, of a people, of a vampire, and of a boy.

In the end, it was love and not fire that saved them.

Thank you so much for reading my series! I hope you enjoyed Kira's story!

If you want to stay up to date with my new releases, sign up for my New Release Newsletter at the link below to receive an email notification every time a new book of mine goes on-sale!

Tinyletter.com/KaitlynDavisBooks

About The Author

Kaitlyn Davis graduated Phi Beta Kappa from Johns Hopkins University with a B.A. in Writing Seminars. She's been writing ever since she picked up her first crayon and is overjoyed to share her work with the world. She currently lives in New York City and dreams of having a puppy of her own.

Connect with the Author Online:

Website:
KaitlynDavisBooks.com
Facebook:
Facebook.com/KaitlynDavisBooks
Twitter:
@DavisKaitlyn
Tumblr:
KaitlynDavisBooks.tumblr.com
Wattpad:
Wattpad.com/KaitlynDavisBooks
Goodreads:
Goodreads.com/author/show/5276341.Kaitlyn_Davis

CPSIA information can be obtained
at www.ICGtesting.com
Printed in the USA
LVOW07s0856250917
549880LV00051B/1456/P